BABYHEAD

BABYHEAD

Kevin Keck

M2 Press

For information email: publisher@m2press.com

Published by M2 Press, North Carolina

First Edition 2018

ISBN: 0692153748
ISBN-13: 978-0692153741

For Everyone
at No Borders No Boundaries Coffee House,
Syracuse, New York, 1997-2000.

"There is a deep, abiding, unshakeable satisfaction in a life of complete failure."

- Edward Abbey

CHAPTER ONE

Morning Wood

WHERE DO I BEGIN?

Well, here it is:

I'm in Paul's room, on his floor, carpet fuzz in my mouth, and what I thought at first was a wicked hangover is actually Paul and his girlfriend, Lourdene, hammering away at each other on his twin bed almost directly above me.

I know there are times when you've got to have it right then, and circumstances can't always be helped, but Paul's mattress is on an old metal frame that's barely holding together, so anytime you move on it the joints moan like six ways of loud. They must know I'm on the floor—they can't think I'm that heavy of a sleeper.

I turn my face upwards. Their bodies are totally under the covers, which kind of sucks, because once or twice I've caught a glimpse of Lourdene with no shirt, and I've always wondered what the rest of the goods were like. Her left leg comes out from under the covers, and her foot dangles over my face—I can see her toes curling and flexing... I usually wake up hard anyway, for one reason or another, but this is too much. I'm tempted to take out the old hog and give him a good working while I enjoy the show, but I'm not a morning person to be honest. I mean, I need to pee in a serious way, and also, I can only masturbate if I'm on my knees. It's a complicated story...

The sad thing is that this is the least frustrating sexual encounter I've had in the last month or so. Paul and Lourdene... they're breaking my heart up there. They wake up, they want to fuck, so they do. It's that simple. Out of all the girls I could have ended up with, my own girlfriend, Megan, had to be a virgin (well, *was* one, anyway), and at 19 even—a veritable Rosetta Stone of sexual discovery these days.

Naturally, when she first told me she had never had sex (we had just finished watching *Before Sunrise*; what it lacks in gratuitous violence it seems to make up for during the post-film hook-up), we were completely naked and I was poised for entry. She put her hands on my face, and looked up at me like she had hurt my feelings and said, "I can't do this unless I know you love me."

Well, what would *you* have done?

Not that we did it anyway. I wasn't even a third of the way in when she screamed like my penis was an iron poker straight from a blacksmith's fire. I was so shaken by her outburst that I immediately lost my bone and rolled off of her and began having heart palpitations. After I calmed down I tried to make some sense of it all, which started with K-Y and ended up with a root beer bottle, neither of which went well.

And it's been like this for the past two months. Every night we start by making out, then we're naked, then I'm going down on her (during which she lies frozen), then she's going down on me, and suddenly she's saying she's *definitely* ready. I know she isn't, but all I'm thinking is that if I don't get rid of my hard-on RIGHT NOW I'm going to wind up with the dreaded blue balls. So I go to slide it in again, things go okay for two seconds, and then she's either crying or screaming. It doesn't matter which. Either way I end up on my back, terrified that I've done some permanent damage with my dick, which may sound arrogant, but hey: it's all I've got.

I know this doesn't sound like much, and maybe it wouldn't be such a big deal if it weren't for the fact that lately everything has just been sucking a giant gonad.

And admittedly, in the grand scheme of things, my life at its worst is still pretty good, but you can't go around thinking like that. It's important to always keep in mind that your problems are the ones that are the most afflicting in the world—if you start realizing that others have it far worse than you, you end up playing Nintendo all day, and spending your nights with your other apathetic friends, watching 80's flicks with feel-good mall montages set to catchy music and wondering why your life isn't overflowing with witty banter and popularity contests easily decided by some serious downhill skiing.

Which is exactly all I've been doing. I mean, not the skiing, but the other stuff...

I spent yesterday afternoon at Megan's while her parents were at work. We started off watching a porn film (*Backdoor Bonanza: Volume XII*) to get ourselves in the mood. I mean, not like we needed much help, but it never hurts. She played it by the book: kissing, nakedness, declarations of moisture and desire, complete agony. Then, in a new chapter she has recently added, tears of guilt at making *my* life such a terror.

We lay there on her bed, holding one another, and I told her not to worry about it. Everything would be okay; these things just take time. I couldn't believe the words were coming out of my mouth even as I said them. What I wanted to say was, *Look: just lay there and like it.* But I've learned that sometimes it's best to just keep things to myself. Besides, Megan has found that the ideal way to alleviate her guilt is by giving me a hand job and letting me come on her. I think this can only lead to a few years of counseling or a serious chemical dependency for her somewhere down the line, but for now it's working. Truth be told, I would probably break up with her and get on with my life if it weren't for a few facts: she's a solid friend of Lourdene and several of the other girls that I know, so I'm just asking for trouble if I break up with her, and also, I have no life to get on with, so there's no point in creating unnecessary problems for myself.

I left her house around five, just before her folks came home, and skated over to Paul's. I don't have a job, thus I can't afford a car, so I get by with my skateboard. And it's tough to get a job when the only way you have to get there is your board. Or the bus, but I don't ride the bus. The few times I did ride it there seemed to be an unspoken code of seating and eye contact that I couldn't quite grasp. I used to get that same vibe in the cafeteria when I was in high school, and I swore when I was out of there I was through with peer related anxiety as it applies to seating. You'd be surprised how much that can limit your activities in life.

I got to Paul's place and walked on in without knocking, which is my usual habit—Paul doesn't lock the door for my sake, which is probably a bad idea where he lives, but he has yet to get me a key. He was there smoking a Camel Light and watching The Learning Channel, which is one of the few pleasures we have in life, especially the show *Connections*, where this English dude explains in each episode how all of our modern technology can be traced back to the invention of the barometer or the horse stirrup.

Paul looked up at me, exasperated.

"Christ. What are we doing here?"

This is a recurring theme in our conversations. We've both lived in Syracuse all our lives, and now that we're out of high school we don't much see the point. In fact, none of our friends do, either. Everyone has a getaway plan; mostly we just lack an excuse. I try to keep it real, though. I know I'm not going anywhere. And I have yet to see anyone else go away, either. It's like every stupid conversation you have, like if you were going to a deserted island and could only take five things, what would they be? Well, who fucking cares? If you're going to end up on a deserted island, odds are you won't have the option to put your five things plan into play, and I seriously doubt too many people will be sitting around under a palm tree all bummed about the fact that they weren't informed beforehand of this little disaster so they could pack their copy of *The Wall* and a Walkman.

"Well, fuck it, dude. Let's go. You've got the money. We'll just get in the car and go." I didn't make an effort to get up.

Paul's grandparents died when he was a senior in high school, and since he was already 18 he picked up a good little chunk of change. I'm not sure how much, but it's been two years and he's managed to halfway support my ass and pay his own bills, plus maintain a girlfriend. He's always said that the money isn't a problem when it comes to leaving, he just doesn't feel like going through the trouble of working his way into another circle of friends. He's all the time trying to get me to go with him, but I figure it's more of a hassle than it's worth. Besides, where would we go? Paul came alive:

"Yeah, let's do it, man. Let's go. Let's just get in the car and go and we'll call everyone when we get there."

"Get where?" I reached over and took the remote and started flipping through the channels. Paul said:

"Who cares? Cali, Florida, Montana... we'll just go. Let's move to Montana. Become dental floss tycoons."

I put on my best Coolio impersonation, "But we ain't got no car!" I stopped at The Game Show Channel. They were showing an old episode of *The Newlywed Game*. Call me crazy, but I like listening to a bunch of badly dressed people say 'making whoopee.'

Paul collapsed back onto the couch.

"Yeah..." He snatched the remote back from me. "Bitch. You think you live here or something?"

So, obviously, we didn't get too far. Our big adventure last night was a constant shuffle from the couch to the refrigerator to Paul's patio out in back of his apartment, associating with the usual suspects: Lourdene; her friends Brenda and Lara; Craig (the one person who actually did leave for a while, but it doesn't count because he came back after three months); and my girlfriend, Megan. Same as every night. Which is fine by me. I don't long for change like Paul does; I've discovered that I like a life built on the sturdy foundation of repetition. I genuinely like these people, we all get on pretty well, and we come from the same place so we're never lost on some inside joke. We made the inside jokes: it's us. It's all the other losers who'll spend the rest of their lives squinting their eyes in our collective direction and half smiling in confusion.

Paul just let out this massive groan, so I assume the bastard is done. I'm looking at the ceiling, hoping they'll just go back to sleep and I can quietly slip out. Paul's face appears above mine, smiling. I say:

"Is that all you've got?"

Lourdene lets out a little squeal.

"You said he was asleep! You fucking liar!"

Paul just keeps on smiling at me, and I can hear Lourdene's fists pounding playfully on his back. He turns back to the bed, and I get up and walk to the bedroom door. Lourdene is still going on about how she thought I was asleep, but you can tell she's not really bothered by it. In fact, I'd almost be willing to bet my board that she's getting all hot again thinking about me watching/listening to them do it. I bet she's wondering if I pleasured myself as well. She wants to be an actress. I know how they are.

I grab my skateboard from where it's leaning against the wall by the front door. Outside it's already so hot and muggy I'm tempted to just go back inside and catch Paul and

Lourdene's second show, but I figure I've had enough weirdness for one day. And it's not even eight o'clock yet.

CHAPTER TWO

A+

I JUMP ON THE BOARD and start kicking it down the street. As I'm getting up enough speed to coast it for a while, I take off my shirt and tie it around my waist. This is ridiculous. It's the end of September and we're in the middle of a heat wave. Any other year they'd be dusting off the salt trucks right now because it usually snows by mid-October. I keep waiting to turn up at my folks' house and find the family slumped over in front of the freezer, dead from the heat. No one around here has a/c, except for Paul, and only because he used some of that inheritance to set himself up right. The rest of the city has been flocking to the malls and the movies. Apparently global warming is good for the retail and entertainment industries.

I turn down Dell Street, then onto Columbus, and down the hill towards Erie Boulevard. My folks live on the Northeast side of town, my friends all live on the Southeast side where the University is (although their association with it is purely geographical), so it can be a real hassle going back and forth, especially on hot mornings. Luckily, going home is mostly downhill.

Just as I'm crossing over East Genesee I realize my bowels feel unsteady. All the PBRs from last night have my intestines in somewhat of an uproar. I kick the board a little faster down the hill and dodge the traffic when I get to Erie, hopping off my board at the median and sprinting across the last two lanes of traffic and into the A-Plus Mart and back towards the bathroom. But I try to be casual once I'm inside the A-Plus; I don't want to be the freak in the convenience store who went running to the can. I try to avoid extreme displays of emotion at all costs, even in the face of impending embarrassment. Enthusiasm, especially when it comes to matters of the toilet, reeks of lameness and a life sheltered by parents (or legal guardians) who shoveled their children full of *Little House on the Prairie* and *Sesame Street*.

Close as I feel to a personal disaster right now, I take time to make sure the door is locked. Then I unroll a series of strips of toilet paper and place them carefully on the toilet seat, making sure that my hands don't come in contact with the tainted porcelain. It takes me a few tries to get strips lengthy enough to go around the seat—the large, industrial roll of paper I'm forced to work with wants to tear off one little square at a time. I also have to abandon one decent strip because as it comes off the roll it grazes the floor, and the only thing I can imagine that could be worse than touching my buttocks to the toilet seat is touching them to this floor.

I barely get myself settled, and as I'm sitting I realize one of my strips is sliding down into the bowl, but it's too late, and I wince at the sting of the coolness that connects with my left cheek.

Normally, I find it difficult to do anything but pee in a public rest room. As a man, standing in front of a urinal, one can assume a casual indifference. But sitting down I just feel so vulnerable. Maybe that's why women have an easier time sharing their feelings with one another: they spend most of their rest room time together in vulnerable positions. I prefer to take care of business such as this at home, with relative silence, and a soothing, low-level lighting effect. Maybe that says something about me on a deeper level, but whatever it is I try my best to just ignore it and push on.

I start to flush the toilet, but unfortunately I've overlooked the fact that I was expecting this fragile piece of plumbing to handle an excess amount of paper, and of course I neglected to give it a complimentary flush, thus lightening its load over two flushes instead of burdening it with one. I decide that an attempt at being sanitary, even when the end result is obviously going to be failure, is better than leaving the situation for the next poor sap. I raise my foot (I never touch a toilet with my hands if I can help it) and bring it down on the handle. I watch, horrified, as the toilet seems to be on the verge of flowing over. I start to take the cover off the tank, to reach in and pull up on the little lever that stops the flow of water, but I don't know how often they clean this toilet. I back away from the bowl and lean against the wall. There's a knock on the door and I quickly look to make sure that it is indeed locked.

"Just a second." When I turn back to the toilet the rising

water has stopped just at the rim.

I look around the bathroom for a plunger. Usually in these single occupancy gas station johns they leave you all the necessities for unforeseen damage. But, of course, not in this one. I wash my hands and stare at the toilet. I kick the lid down with my foot, grab my board and unlock the door and step out. A guy in a suit is looking impatiently at his watch.

"It's about time."

"Whatever," and I walk away.

Suddenly I feel the serious threat of hunger. I didn't get a chance to eat anything last night before I sacked out, except a half a bag of Doritos. I stride up to the counter. I see a pair of hands taking last night's pizza slices out of the warmers. This girl steps out from behind the food warmers that line the counter and she stares at me, and I'd swear she just hung the moon.

She brushes her red hair behind her ear, tilts her head and looks up at me, not smiling, but kind of soft.

"You want something?"

I don't say anything. I can't. I swear I can hear a choir of angels and a band of heavenly hosts sending up hallelujahs somewhere. In the back of my head I have this vague notion that I'm in serious trouble. Then I feel a hand on my shoulder.

"Yeah, I want something." The guy from the bathroom comes right up beside me and looks me in the eyes. I shrug his hand off my shoulder. He leans on the counter with his knuckles, a real champion. He says:

"This punk crapped all over the Goddamned bathroom and stopped up the toilet and I had to piss in the sink."

"Hey man: my crap was in the bowl. Totally."

The guy turns and puts his index finger right dead center in my chest. I think about stepping back, but I don't want to look like a pussy, so I move forward. Or try to. The guy has strong fingers.

"Look, I had to piss in the sink. Where do I wash my hands, huh?" To underscore his point, he says again, "Huh?"

The guy takes his finger out of my chest and turns and looks at the girl standing behind the counter. I look down at her breasts. Fantastic. Her name tag says: *Hi, I'm here to serve you. My name is Lia.* 'Lia' is printed in big letters with a red marker, and the 'i' is dotted with a smiley face. Classic.

"Well," the guy says. "What are we going to do about this?"

Lia looks at me, then back at Knuckles.

"I can't believe you peed in our sink. That's gross. I mean, urine is sterile, but it's gross. Get out."

"Are you serious?" The guy's knuckles are going white.

She doesn't say anything. She looks serious. Knuckles looks serious too. I probably don't look serious at all, though. Most likely I appear to be guilty. I think I often look guilty, regardless of the situation or my innocence. It's something I've learned to live with.

Knuckles looks at me, squints his eyes up, then walks out. I look back at Lia and say:

"Hey, cool."

She walks a few feet away and bends down behind the counter and comes back up with a plunger.

"Here. Make sure it goes down this time."

* * *

After about five minutes I get the toilet running smoothly again.

I figure by now it must be around 8:30, which means my dad should be in the bed when I get home, and mom should be long gone. Mom works during the day as a secretary at the University, and dad works third shift at Carrier, making air conditioners or something related to them. Which is ironic when you consider that the one big factory remaining in this town produces something everyone could use right now but which no one has. I don't see either of my folks much, which is fine by me, because all dad does is harass me about getting a job and mom just wants me to go to college since I can go for free to the university because she works there. The only person I do see with any regularity is my younger sister, and I'd just as soon avoid her too. In recent years my family has become less like a family and more like four unfortunately paired roommates.

I walk out of the bathroom wondering why I just don't move in with Paul or something since I'm there most of the time anyway. Going home everyday, or most everyday, to uncertain circumstances, where I don't know if I'll be defending my right to be unemployed, uneducated, or just to be a loser (my sister is a little more general in explaining to me what my problem is) surely doesn't help the surly state of my bowels. But moving all my stuff would be such a hassle. I have 20 years of stuff, most of it under my bed and in my closet, and I don't throw anything away, ever. I'm not sure what good a program from the Harlem Globetrotters' visit to Syracuse in 1985 will do in the future, but I'm willing to find out at this point in the game.

I wonder if there's any Pepto at the house. Someone says:

"What the fuck?"

I look around the store. The girl—Lia—is standing at the top of the aisle staring at the floor. She looks up at me, glaring:

"Are you an absolute dildo?"

This sounds like a trick question so I keep my mouth shut.

"Look." She stretches her arm out, palm up, and tilts her head looking behind me. When I don't immediately turn around, she looks at me again making a twirling motion with her index finger. I turn. There is a trail of dirty water leading from the bathroom door to where I'm standing on the white tiled floor. I suddenly realize I have the plunger in my hands. I look back at Lia and try to smile, but instead I just nod and walk back to the bathroom with my head down, put the plunger by the toilet, and go back out to ask her for a mop. She's waiting for me with one in her hand. She doesn't say anything, just shakes her head as I take it from her, and goes back behind the counter.

I mop up the dirty water from the rest room and down the aisle, then lean the mop over in the corner at the end of the counter. I go up to the register. Lia has her back to me, putting a new bag in the garbage can behind the counter. Dave Matthews is playing on the radio, and Lia is shaking her hips a little. She's petite, but not in a waif-like, strung out kind of way; she has curves. Curves are good. She turns around, looks at me like she's never seen me before, or like she wasn't expecting me to be behind her, just staring. She raises an eyebrow.

"Yes?"

I really don't have anything prepared to say. So I say:

"I left the mop over there."

"Good boy."

I look at the neat stacks of lighters that are next to the register. There's even a rectangular piece of cardboard with buttons pinned to it that declare lame sentiments such as: *Take this job and shove it* and *These boots were made for knockin'*. She says:

"Anything else?"

I muster up as much suaveness as I can at such an early hour:

"Got a couple of slices left for me?"

"No. I threw them all out," she says flatly.

"Well..."

Lia shakes her head and turns and then walks away into some back room behind the counter. Dave sings of the frailty of existence. My stomach churns slowly. Maybe an ultra-smooth cat would leave his number on the counter, but that same ultra smooth character wouldn't have clogged the toilet either. I grab my board from where it's been leaning against the counter and walk out the door, then start kicking it back to my parents' place. I'm hungry and I have that awful raunchy feeling you get sometimes after a night of drinking too much. I just want to go back to bed. Also, I want to wash my ass.

CHAPTER THREE

News Flash

MY DAD IS SITTING AT the kitchen table eating breakfast and watching the last bit of *Good Morning America* on the black and white portable TV. He doesn't even look at me when I walk in, just keeps shoveling forks full of fried egg into his mouth while watching some woman who's talking about the breast implants she got after she had a mastectomy. I should've known.

Mom had cancer a few years back and lost her left breast. She wanted to lose the other and just get implants, but we didn't have the money, and insurance wouldn't pay for the fakes, so she just has the one breast now and wears this plastic thing in her bra so it gives the appearance of her having two healthy, God fearing, American mammories. But since her surgery dad has become obsessed with breast augmentation. He behaves just like he did when he was shopping for a new VCR when I was in sixth grade. I mean, basically he's comparison shopping, just waiting until he finds a deal within his price range. I'd be willing to say that my father is perhaps the foremost expert on breast augmentation between New York City and Buffalo. And also that if he came upon a roadside tragedy where a woman's life hung in the balance and hinged on her having successful implant surgery right then, dad could probably do it on the spot, or at least give a decent set of instructions on how to proceed.

I grab some juice out of the refrigerator, pour myself a small glass and stand behind dad while the woman on TV talks about her self-esteem since the surgery. Dad says:

"Whatcha think those are?"

I look at the woman's chest—she's wearing a tight knit shirt, and if this were a full size screen it might be impressive, but as it stands they can't be more than a centimeter or so big. But I give it a shot anyway.

"I don't know. Maybe a c-cup."

Dad sips his coffee.

"No, I mean what do you think they're made of?"

"Well, what? Silicone?"

"Son, don't you know what goes on in the world outside of your head? Silicone is out—company that made them went bankrupt because the implants leaked and made the women sick."

"Oh."

"Soy."

"Like the burger?"

"Absolutely. Amazing stuff, isn't it? They say it looks and feels better than the silicone ones. Maybe even better than real breasts." Dad puts down his coffee and beams, rubbing his hands together. "I tell you Jordan, I see things like this happening in the world, and I swear to you I'm just lucky to be alive to witness it. These are exciting times!"

I try to muster a smile, but at my age the girls still have naturally perky breasts so the joy of the moment is somewhat lost on me. Dad nods his head and starts cutting up bits of Spam with clinical precision and running it through the remaining yolk left on his plate. I put my glass in the sink and walk down the hall to the bathroom. The door is shut. I knock politely. When no one answers I knock again with authority.

"Kelly, are you in there?"

Dad's voice comes down the hall before she can answer.

"Jordan! Don't you and your sister start. And I want you to go and apply for a job at no fewer than five places today."

I whisper to the door:

"Hurry up. Slut."

Dad says:

"You hear me, Jordan?"

"Yeah." Dad pokes his head in the hall:

"Don't 'yeah' me—just do it. You either need to start paying some rent here, or get out." He disappears back into the kitchen. The bathroom door opens a little and Kelly says:

"Douchebag."

She shuts the door. I go to my room and kick off my shoes and flop on my bed. I have the vague impression I can smell my own butt, which isn't pleasant at all, so I move from my bed to the floor just in case the smell has the potential to cling.

I'm staring at this blank spot on my wall. It's not actually blank, like white or anything. There's this yellow, orange, and brown plaid wallpaper showing through. My parents put it up when I was five. I remember this very clearly because when they weren't looking I ate some of the paste and became violently ill.

Anyway, I was in seventh grade when I finally hit my limit for looking at this wretched wallpaper. I started putting up posters. Not just random posters either. I took my time deciding what should go on my walls. I only put up graven images of people I really like or things I seriously stand behind. Sometimes, in light of new information, a poster might come down. I've taken my Charlie Manson poster down twice, but last year it went back up again. As far as I can tell, he's in prison simply for what he thinks, which is bullshit. That's like putting him in jail for not crying at his mother's funeral. Of course he did compel some of his followers to kill innocent people in a brutal fashion. I don't know—Manson is a tough call.

Anyway, I've got my room covered, walls and ceiling, with posters, except for that one spot, because this room is really my Zen rock garden. I read a *G.I. Joe* comic book in which a Zen master took thirty years to place the last rock in his garden because he wanted it to be perfection. (I wish I could find that comic now... I'd really like to know that Zen master's name; unfortunately, despite the fact that I don't throw things away, my mom will occasionally stage a guerrilla attack on stuff she thinks I don't need any more and dispatch it mercilessly to the curb on trash day—I figure I've lost thousands of dollars worth of baseball cards that way.)

I envision myself as practicing my own form of misguided Zen. Zen teaches that you should achieve enlightenment by giving up your attachment to the world of things, which I've done: I have no job, no car, no house of my own. I live on the goodwill of friends and family. To be truly enlightened, I think you eventually have to give up even the *desire* to give up your attachment to the world. Or something like that. Someone could argue that I'll never become enlightened since I'm attached to completing my poster garden but that's the thing about Zen: it's a paradox. I don't plan on taking 30 years to finish this wall either. I'm sure my parents will have kicked me out long before I become that much of a loser. My goal is a year. After that I don't know. Right now I only have the time to concentrate on one quest. When I'm finally done with looking at this ridiculous wallpaper that's haunted me for fifteen years, maybe then I can set my sights on another personal grail.

My dad steps in my room:

"Don't you and your sister get started. I'm going to bed."

I sit up from where I'm lying on the floor, apparently looking guilty (again), ready to defend myself before I've committed any offense.

"Hey—"

But I don't get a chance to say anything else before he shuts the door to my room.

I hear Kelly come out of the bathroom and go down the hall towards the kitchen. I make a break for it. Usually, Kelly isn't the type to linger in the can, but she will if she thinks I need in there. I keep wondering what I did to her in her youth to make her hate me so much.

I turn on the shower and strip my clothes off and toss them in the hamper. I check myself out in the mirror. I look like hammered shit. No wonder I couldn't get that girl at the A-Plus Mart to give me the time of day.

Thinking about her now, I feel a stirring at my center that I haven't felt in at least an hour or so. Maybe now is the time to put to rest those urges that Paul and Lourdene forced upon me so early this morning. Usually at this time my stiff self is just nuzzling me awake against the floor of Paul's apartment (and peacefully, too, I might add), or his couch, and on those odd occasions, my own bed. And even then I rise only briefly before shrinking back to sleep.

I imagine going back to the A-Plus Mart tomorrow—I can see her there in those awful teal polo shirts the employees have to wear, and her breasts are perky, and I'm wondering what they look like under her shirt. Perhaps I will say to her, *So, what's in that little room behind the counter there?* and she'll say, *Well, come back here and I'll show you.* (It is the most pathetic of porn plots, I know, but I am just a simple man...) I hop the counter and follow her into the room, shutting the door behind us. She isn't surprised by this. In fact it's what she was hoping for. I grab her and press my tongue into her mouth. She says to me, *Stop. I hate foreplay. Just do me.* I swoon with desire. We are both suddenly naked. She looks down between my legs, says:

"Oh God!"

But it isn't her voice at all. I turn to the door and Kelly is just standing there, staring at me, and I scream:

"SHUT THE DOOR!"

It comes out more choked than that, though, because I am a man in the grip of ecstasy—ecstasy letting loose onto the sink and the mirror. Kelly stands there slack jawed, then slams the door, muffling her audible disgust. I lean on the sink and I want to cry. Dad's door opens quickly, shaking the entire house.

"Goddammit!"

I don't hear anything for a second, then I hear him walking down the hall and he knocks on the bathroom door. I turn away quickly in case he decides to come barging in as well. Fortunately, my dad is a man respectful of the sanctity of the toilet.

"Jordan? What did you do to her?"

"Nothing."

"Jordan?"

"I said nothing."

I hear him walk back down the hallway and knock on Kelly's door:

"Kelly? What happened."

I'm waiting for it. I figure this will probably be the last straw, but I can't quite envision getting kicked out of my house for beating off. I mean, I know the old man must do it, and isn't there some honor amongst men? He and mom haven't had sex since her operation (as far as I can tell) and that was years ago. There's no way he's not at least giving it a basic maintenance whack every so often. Not that my parents were bunnies or anything, but it was obvious when they had stoked the cooling embers of middle aged desire: they doted on each other for at least 48 hours following their romps. These days they don't even seem to touch.

I press my ear to the bathroom door:

"It was nothing dad. I saw a spider," Kelly says, sounding genuinely frightened.

I don't hear my father make s sound, so I imagine he's giving my sister the look of *Come on—you don't expect me to believe that, do you?* But either he does believe, or he's just so tired he doesn't care, because after a few seconds I hear him move on and both of their doors shut. I don't know how I feel about having my most precious self referred to as "a spider."

I clean up, give myself a good washing, and when I'm done and dried I go to my room and collapse on the bed. I get up before I doze off, though, and put DJ Shadow on the stereo. Also, I lock the door.

I'm standing in the kitchen watching the portable. I was asleep a few minutes ago, dreaming there were helicopters circling the house and voices shouting at me to drop my penis and come out with my hands up. Through the blinds I could see the neighbors and news cameras hungry to get a look at "The Masturbator." But it was just in my head. Except for the helicopters. They are really making a racket.

My local anchor explains the situation: on Crouse Avenue, up by the university and the hospital, someone has driven a Ford Pinto through the front doors of the McDonald's and started shooting up the place. There's footage of idle police cars blocking the streets. Apparently no one has been hurt, but the guy driving the Pinto is holding hostages and refuses to talk to the police. Like anything real, the events are unfolding far too slow for live coverage, and the station keeps cutting back and forth to the distant video of motionless police cars and our local anchorman who keeps assuring us that we viewers will be continually updated on the unfolding tragedy. But as far as I can tell, and from what the news reports, no one has been hurt, so the only tragedy seems to be that McDonald's will be closed for a while due to repairs.

Mom walks in carrying a bag of groceries.

"Hi hon. There's another bag in the car—would you mind getting it?"

"What are you doing home? Are you cooking?"

"Your father has boxing tonight, remember? I wasn't going to cook, but I can make you some Hamburger Helper if you want. Have you seen the news? They closed the school for the rest of the day."

Mom doesn't cook much anymore, but when she does cook it's always Hamburger Helper. She used to make real meals, back when we all used to eat together, when Kelly and I were still in school. But not long after mom's operation my dad started refereeing boxing matches a couple nights a week at a gym as a favor to his best friend, and mom goes over to watch Must See TV with one of her friends on Thursdays, so there's hardly any reason for her to fix anything for us as a family unit. I tell her not to worry about it, that I'll grab something on my own since I'm going out later anyway.

I open the passenger door on the old Honda hatchback and take the groceries up into my arms. I start to close the door, but I see my mom's purse sitting in the floorboard. I sit the groceries on the roof of the car and lean inside and open the purse. Usually, if I need money, I'll just borrow it from Paul, but I owe the guy nearly three grand after several years of steady borrowing. And I don't know where I'll get the money to pay him back. The guy is a prince though—never says a word about it, and when I mention it he just tells me to get it to him when I can. Regardless, I'd prefer not to push my tab up much more.

Why do women have so much stuff in their purses? I haven't come across any money yet, and already I have a small pile of shit laying on the floorboard. I poke my head up to see if my mom is looking outside, suspiciously, but she's not. I look in my hand; I'm holding birth control pills.

I only know what they are because my sister takes them to regulate her cycle. Generally, it's my policy to never think about my sister's vagina, but a guy I went to high school with made it known to me that he didn't have to wear a jimmy when he scrogged my sister because she was on the pill due to the fact that her period was irregular. And quite honestly, that's the only reason I can imagine my mom would take these. Like I said, she and my dad don't even hug each another any more. Unless, of course, she's got a side piece. Which is ridiculous. My mom still buys me and my sister Easter baskets every year. Any woman who does that after her kids are past the age of eight is a saint. I realize I'm holding something directly related to the function of my mother's vagina and a chill goes through me. I toss them on the pile of junk on the floorboard, and by some stroke of luck put my hands on a loose twenty floating in the bottom of her purse. Solid gold.

When I step back in the house mom is opening a box of

Macaroni Hamburger Helper. She says:

"Did you hear about that man at the McDonald's? Isn't that just the saddest thing?"

"I'm going out tonight. What's so sad about it?"

"So no hamburger helper?"

"I already told you that. I'm going back to bed."

"I'm sorry. Do you need any money, sweetie?"

"Actually—no. I'm good."

CHAPTER FOUR

Please Drive Through

BY SEVEN MY DAD HAS gone to referee boxing and I'm awake again and kicking it over to Paul's. I pass a series of houses, kids running around in the street, adults out on the front porches, most of them just talking or sipping on 40s wrapped in brown paper bags. I always feel like they're staring at me when I cruise past. Which is stupid, I suppose—sometimes it's hard to believe I'm not the center of the world. It's like this nearly every day. I ride past the same houses, and the only thing different is the number of people who stare back at me. Even in the winter, when my balls are so cold I can practically hear them rattle, there always seems to be someone watching me mope by. Sometimes I think they're hoping it won't be me, and then they can think about other things for a while because something will have finally changed.

I mentioned to Paul one time how I felt completely scrutinized, hoping he would put my paranoia to rest. Instead, he said:

"Hey, baby, you're dealing with trapped people here. You think any of them have any more prospects than another day of the same solid shit? You don't endear yourself to them zipping back and forth with your carefree sugar-free self."

Craig and Paul are smoking and watching CNN with the closed captioning on; they're kicking it old school tonight with Ice Cube's *The Predator* pushing out a low rumble on the stereo. No one looks in my direction when I walk in. The girls (minus my girlfriend) are huddled in the kitchen talking quietly amongst themselves. When I sit down opposite Paul and Craig, the girls erupt with laughter.

I get up, cross over to Paul, and take one of his cigarettes from his pack. Paul says:

"Bitch, you're blocking the TV."

"What's up?"

"This shit at McDonald's baby. Haven't you heard what this whacky motherfucker is up to?"

"Killing people?"

Paul looks away from the television and lights a cigarette as he says:

"This fucker is crazy dude, not psychotic. He's not killing anyone. He just sent out all the hostages with bags full of Big Macs for all the cops who've been standing around all day."

"But I think it should be noted," Craig says, "that this was not a completely benevolent act. He did not send them beverages or fries."

Paul nods thoughtfully. Then:

"Still, this dude is whack. Do you seriously not know what is going on?"

"My mom was watching *Wheel of Fortune* when I left the house—you know the news can't compete with that."

"Your mom is fucked up."

Craig says:

"Yeah."

"Anyway," Paul says, stubbing out his cigarette before it's halfway done (something he only does when he's really excited), "this nutty bitch drives his Pinto—a fucking Pinto! Can you believe it?—he drives this thing through the front doors of McDonald's and jumps out of his car and starts shooting. But he doesn't shoot anybody. He just shoots, and so people are scared shitless. So he tells everyone to stay where they are, and then he tells the McDonald's peeps to start cooking. And not just cook anything—he wants those fools cooking enough Fillets-o-Fish and McNuggets to load up his car. One of the hostages was just interviewed and unloaded all that info. They'll show it again in a sec." Paul fires up another cigarette.

"Are you serious?"

"Fuck yeah he's serious," Craig says. "You think shit this weird could just be made up? This is the real deal, man. This is a dude with guns and hostages and a Pinto full of fast food. It doesn't get anymore real than this."

I say:

"Shit."

The girls' laughter comes wafting out of the kitchen again. I ask:

"So what's this guy going to do with all this food?"

"That's what we're waiting to see, baby," Paul says. Craig offers:

"I think he's pissed cheeseburgers don't cost a quarter anymore and he's taking back what's his."

"So why isn't he making them cook cheeseburgers?"

"Oh. Yeah. Maybe they don't keep as well as fish and chicken."

I go:

"Let's play Mario Kart," I say.

Craig and Paul both frown at me. I head into the kitchen. The girls immediately stop talking. I say:

"Where's Megan?"

"She said she'd meet us later," Laura says flatly.

"Where?"

"Wherever."

I have the distinct feeling I'm not really wanted here. I grab a Utica Club out of the fridge and head onto the back patio.

This might sound lame but sometimes I like to just chill at night on someone's porch, or wherever—sometimes even during the day—and just stare up at the trees and think, you know. And what's stupid is I really don't think about too much, at least not any one particular thing. I feel like a movie camera when I do it, like the first thing I see is my opening shot, and then a little story starts to unfold. Usually my opening shot is of the moon glimpsed through tree branches, but there's no moon tonight. At least not one I can see. In fact, I can only see the radio tower at the University on the top of Mt. Olympus (so named because it's the highest point on campus).

In the camera of my mind there's this radio tower you can see through the branches of pine trees. The camera pans down toward the base of the tower where there are dorms, but all the windows are dark because it's summer and no one is in them yet. But one by one the lights in the dorm start to come on, and the picture becomes time lapse photography. People are moving in and out of view quickly in the windows. You can't possibly watch all of them so you have to focus on a few. Someone has on a brightly colored shirt, another is naked every once in a while, but everyone is moving so fast that they all look essentially the same. They're just a blur of people, of lives converging. And of course you can see some trees at the edge of the dorms, so you know when the seasons are changing, and then it starts to snow, but the people are always there, always moving in and out of view, coming and going, but we don't know anything about them. The only story you ever get is just them coming and going and the seasons, and in summer there's not so many people—maybe a janitor skulks by each window, flipping on lights and checking things out, and you feel so lonely watching him make his way through this big building all by himself. Maybe his is the only story you feel connected to because you see him long enough to realize that this is his job, and it must not be much of a life at all. You see him a couple of times, always alone, always making the same solitary journey in and out of each room, just in the middle of Spring when the blossoms are starting to fall off the trees, and just before Autumn, when all the people come back. And you've watched, you realize, this same thing happening over and over for like what must be, in this space of compressed time, like 10 years. But nothing changes. You start to pick up subtle things—the people who fall on top of one another for a few seconds, people pointing at one another in various windows before one leaves and the other throws up his or her hands. But there's another thing, something you don't notice the first few times. The radio tower—there's these little charges of electricity running up the tower and as soon as they reach the top they vanish into the sky. You don't know what to make of this when you first see it: the blur of people, the lonely janitor, the sudden coming and going of seasons, and then you realize that the electricity is there only in Spring, and it's all these people, the ones that are done, disappearing into the world. You see clouds gathering around the radio tower, and the voltage is rippling along it. Then the camera pans around and you see this lightning flashing down, but far away. Over Syracuse, there's just dull gray clouds, with only the threat of a storm. That's it.

Which is exactly how I've felt living here for the last couple of years. I watch these punks come in from all over, and they spend four years here just goofing off, date raping one another, getting plastered, doing lines off one another's stomachs and trashing the town, and then they get their ticket to the world and they're off to become *captains of industry* or some such birthright.

My sister worked for a day at the university in one of the dining halls. She said after two hours of listening to the students complain about the food, or their cars, or the amount of money their parents sent them, she freaked and left, which caused the line to back up and out of the dining hall and down the block because no one in line, for some reason, could dish out their own food. The dining hall supervisor had to come down and do it to get things going again. Or so my mom says.

Between this, and my girlfriend with her vaginal issues, and the need for a job, not to mention that whole thing at the A-Plus Mart this morning—Christ, that girl just smoked every girl I've seen lately—you know, a guy could get really bummed.

Which, admittedly, I am.

I've been down a lot lately. I don't think I used to be like this.

Mom has pictures all over the house of me and my sister when we were little. Like, at least from when we were babies up until we were both teenagers, and then I guess my sister and I both started getting weird about having our pictures taken. Maybe it was acne. Who knows? Anyway, after about 1990 there's not so many pictures, except for the ones we had taken at school for the yearbook and whatever.

But in all these pictures of when we're kids we're always laughing. I don't remember ever being the morose wet blanket I am now. I mean, after mom got sick, sure, I wasn't exactly a happy little camper. But that's really the first time I can recall being seriously depressed. That afternoon when I came home from school and I saw that dad was home—this was before he worked the night shift at Carrier, when he was working first shift at the GM plant before it closed down—I knew something was terribly wrong. My dad doesn't miss work ever. Kelly was already home as well, and she came running up to me when I walked through the door and hugged me. That was the next indication that something wasn't right; Kelly and I had been on bad terms for several months at that point, probably because I hated having to go to school with my little sister who heard about whatever I did and told mom and dad, and she was most likely just as embarrassed by me. I had a ridiculous haircut at the time, shaved on the sides and long on top, and dyed green. It's not something I'm proud of now, but we're family, after all, and I figure if your own sister can't forgive you for wanting to express yourself in the most idiotic of ways then who can?

Still, I hugged her back, though I don't think I knew for sure why. I just knew things were about to get rough. I looked past Kelly, over to the kitchen table, where mom and dad were sitting solemnly. Dad had mom's hands in his, and he looked up at me, and it was the first time I ever saw him cry. I know that's some touchy-feely *After School Special* bullshit, but it's the truth. Like I said, this is a guy who never misses work.

Later that day I was sitting in my room by myself, and I could hear mom and dad in their room talking, but I couldn't make out what they were saying. I started thinking about how many times I had gone to sleep like that, listening to their murmur, and I couldn't imagine what it would be like to be lying there in my room, unable to drift off to the two of them making their end of the day idle chit chat. I mean, it's been years since I fell asleep to the sound of them, because of dad's work schedule and the fact that I rarely sleep there anymore, and even before that I usually had the radio on or something, but I liked having that option. I tried to think of what it would be like if mom died, the miserable silence that would just consume the house at night. It's sort of turned out like that anyway. But yeah. I used to be a real barrel of monkeys. Now?

Not so much.

"Cheer up, buttercup."

I look up and Megan is standing in the doorway, smiling. I go:

"I didn't hear you come out."

"Surprised?" She leans down to kiss me.

"Always... I thought you were meeting us out?"

Megan sits down beside me and takes a pack of Marlboro Lights out of her jeans pocket.

"I was going to, you know, because I was going to go to Chuck's with Abby—" Abby is one of Megan's "other friends," an elusive bunch of people that she is always talking about, but people that I am not entirely convinced exist, much like Snufflupagus in his first few years plaguing Big Bird (though no one I know recalls the time when Snufflupagus was considered by the rest of the *Sesame Street* cast to be just a figment of Big Bird's imagination; could I have dreamed it all, a Bizarro World *Sesame Street*?) "—but when I call Abby to come pick me up she's like, *No way, haven't you seen the news?* Which I hadn't, and I have now, and I just don't get it, you know, I mean, shit like this is happening all the time. It's so fucking last year. Just shoot the guy and get it over with because how are we supposed to get down to Chuck's with all those police cars there? And you know with the police all around they're going to probably be real anal about carding everyone."

Uninterested as I am in a guy filling his Pinto up with overly-processed fish and chicken, I'm not as dismissive of it all as Megan is:

"Yeah, but Meg, this stuff doesn't happen all the time around here."

"I know? Like isn't that the most beat thing about it? You know this kind of crazy is completely lame when it finally comes to Syracuse. Even the psychos in this town are just so dated." She blows out a long stream of smoke from between her lips.

I want to say to her, *You are one fucked up chick and I'm just now realizing that, which makes me feel like a complete asshole*, but I don't have the energy for that kind of confrontation. Besides, I've told her that I love her, and that obligates me to some amount of tolerance, so instead I say:

"You know, people could be killed."

I think she's about to laugh, in which case I will have to muster up the energy to explain to her just how mental she is, but she smiles at me and says:

"You're so cute when you think about other people. It's one of the things that I really like about you, like the way you think about me so much. It just makes me all giggly." She leans over and kisses my cheek, then presses her lips to my ear and says softly, "You know what? I think tonight's the night."

She turns my face to hers with her hand on my cheek, and gives me one of her patented seductive looks. I try to look enthused; I can already feel the anxiety building toward when she starts screaming about how much my penis pains her. This isn't helping me one bit.

Paul is yelling inside, and I realize that the low rumble of the stereo that was just a dull throbbing outside has stopped.

"WHAT THE FUCK? YOU FUCKERS HAVE GOT TO COME

SEE THIS SHIT!"

I don't rush inside, and when Megan and I get to the living room everyone is staring at the television in awe.

"What happened?"

Paul turns the volume up.

On the television the view of the McDonald's in from above, I'm guessing from a helicopter. S.W.A.T. team guys are rushing the place with their guns drawn, and the newscaster is trying his best to articulate what a tense moment this is. He stops speaking for a moment. Then he resumes by announcing that there are unconfirmed reports that the assailant inside has been shot, either by the police or himself. Megan chirps:

"See? Finally."

I think I'm the only one who hears. She loops her arms around mine and presses her body up against me, raises up on her tiptoes and kisses my cheek. I smile, but I don't mean to, and I'm pissed that I do it. To make up for it I pull away from her and sit down on the floor. She sits down next to me and kisses my neck and leans her head on my shoulder. I feel myself starting to smile again. Paul says:

"Okay. Let's go."

No one says anything. He mutes the television.

"What's up? Let's go."

"What do you mean let's go?" Brenda says. "What kind of a dumbass are you? I want to see what happens."

"That's what I'm talking about. Let's go down there and see what's going on." Paul stands up and turns off the TV. Lara says:

"Are you crazy?"

"Look, this is some serious shit. Let's go check it out. It's like a mile away. We're going to sit here and watch it go down on TV?"

Craig gets up and goes into the kitchen and comes back with a beer in each of the pockets of his shorts and one in each hand:

"Let's rock."

"I don't think this is a good idea," I say.

Megan grabs my hand:

"Come on, it'll be fun." Then to no one in particular: "Do you think we'll be able to get down to Chuck's?"

We're standing around outside the Tri-Delt house on Walnut Avenue, along with a couple hundred other people, a full two blocks from where all the action is. A few houses down some frat boys have put their stereo speakers in the window and are blasting Sublime.

There are guys across the street throwing a Frisbee, and nearly everyone has a beer in hand. I can smell hamburgers cooking—that seems in poor taste under the circumstances. It's dark and the lights from the news helicopters are blinding as they sweep over the crowd. If you had managed to avoid your television all day you'd swear a party was under way. I find it rather disorienting.

"This sucks." Paul is pacing back and forth.

"What?" No one else seems to be listening to him. The girls are a few feet away, sitting in a circle on the street and smoking. Craig keeps walking up and down the sidewalk, drinking his beers, informing me and Paul of how great this all is every time he passes us.

"I can't see a thing, dude. And why doesn't anyone have the news playing out here? What gives? No one would be out here if this wasn't going down, so doesn't anyone want to know what the scoop is?"

I can't listen to what Paul is saying. I mean, I can, but there's just all these chattering voices right now, all this laughing—I'm not really cool with being here. I can feel my heart starting to race a little. I realize we're in the middle of a serious amount of people with no easy and clear way out. Yeah. I'm not too thrilled about this.

"Fuck yeah, fuck-o's! This is the fucking shit!" Craig is giving me and Paul a thumbs-up as he cruises past again.

I feel someone tug on my sleeve. Megan kisses me as soon as I turn my head. Then she whimpers:

"Is this ever going to be through? We'll never get to Chuck's like this."

"I don't think we're going to make it to Chuck's tonight, Meg."

"Are you serious?"

I open my mouth to tell her that I am, in fact, completely serious, and that if she needs to have this verified to her at this point in the game then she a righteous idiot.

"Meg, I am completely—" a Frisbee eclipses my view of Megan's face and has its flight halted by the bridge of her nose. She immediately collapses in tears, which would normally send me into an emotional panic because I never know what to say when someone cries, but I am already in an emotional panic. Paul says:

"What the fuck happened?"

"I don't know man. This Frisbee just came out of nowhere. It just, you know, took her down." I start turning around, trying to see where the Frisbee came from. The guys a little ways off are still chucking their disc back and forth, so it wasn't them.

Brenda jumps up from where she is sitting and comes over to Megan. She looks up at me and says:

"What did you do to her?"

I almost get pissed that I would be implicated, but then I realize that I'm probably looking guilty again. I say:

"This frisbee... it just came out of nowhere..." I look up at the sky where the helicopters are stirring the air. I ponder the possibility for a moment that a reporter in a fit of boredom threw a frisbee at the crowd just to see what would happen, but then I remember (again) that my friends and I are not the center of the world.

Suddenly other girls appear and huddle around Megan and our girls. I forget that I'm supposed to be looking for the cowboy who doesn't have control of his disc and instead watch as these strangers calm Megan. They stroke her hair and talk to her in tones too low for me to hear with all the other noise going on. Before I know what has happened the other girls have taken Megan, Lourdene, Lara and Brenda into the Tri-Delt house. Paul is still scanning the crowd and I say:

"Dude, we have to get out of here."

"What?" He turns around. "Where did the girls go?"

"Into the Tri-Delt house. These other girls just came out of nowhere—"

"They're inside?"

"Yes. These girls—"

Paul looks as if he's about to say something else, and then he doesn't, and he stands there running his hand over the back of his neck. I say:

"Dude, something has been off about this day from the beginning. Waking to you and Lourdene having sex, this guy in the pinto, I stopped up a toilet at the A-Plus and Kelly caught me jerking..."

"You got caught jerking by your sister?"

"Yeah."

"Man." Paul rubs the back of his neck again and shakes his head. "That is the weirdest. What did you say?"

"I told her to shut the door."

"That was probably a wise response."

"But yeah, it was weird. It's all been weird today. And now the girls are in a sorority house. When is this madness going to stop?"

A guy beside Paul and me says:

"Cool. You found our disc."

Paul and I turn at the same time, but there's no one there. I don't remember smoking any weed tonight, but I rub my eyes anyway and I look again.

Paul says:

"Uh."

A midget is standing in front of us with a plastic cup of beer in his hand. He's wearing Birkenstocks and these shorts which were obviously designed for someone on the verge of entering first grade. He has a tattoo above his right nipple: a stick of dynamite with a cartoonish explosion emanating from it which says *"KA-BOOM!"*. The midget says:

"Can I get my disc back?"

"Dude, you need to be more careful with this. You hit his girlfriend in the face." I'm amazed by Paul's composure.

"Seriously? Shit dude, I'm sorry." He holds out his hand. "Seriously, man, I'm seriously fucking sorry. I'm just, you know..." He raises the beer cup in his other hand. I say:

"You could have broken her nose. It is broken for all I know." I'm surprised at how pissed I sound after I've said this. The midget takes a step back.

"Dude, seriously... I'm sorry. I mean, dude..." and he trips over the leg of a guy standing behind him. As I watch him fall all I can think is *Does that hurt him as much as it hurts me to fall? He doesn't have as far to go to the ground...* But it doesn't matter if he gets hurt falling or not because the guy he tripped over falls too and lands right on top of the midget.

The guy gets up immediately and looks as puzzled as Paul and I do. All the people around us look down at the midget. The guy says to the midget:

"Jerry, you okay?" But Jerry doesn't say anything; he's had the wind knocked out of him. The guy turns to us:

"Hey, what the fuck did you do to Jerry?"

"Nothing man. He hit my friend's girlfriend in the face with his disc, and we were just telling him to be more careful."

Another guy steps forward:

"Oh, so by telling him to be more careful you decided you'd kick his ass because he's smaller than you two faggots."

I have the distinct feeling that my natural look of guilt is about to work against me in a big way. I realize that a crowd of frat boys is forming in a very hostile manner. Paul steps forward:

"I didn't lay a finger on Tattoo. He tripped."

"So you're making fun of his tattoo now, huh?" The guy that toppled on the midget is pointing vigorously at me and Paul. "You know what that tattoo means? It was bestowed on him by the loyal brothers of Delta Kappa Epsilon because big bangs come in small packages."

Paul looks at me.

"I think you mean big *things* come in small packages."

"You making fun of Jerry again, bright boy? You think we don't know what we mean? We mean *big bangs*. All the ladies love Jerry. They say he fucks like a little rabbit all night. Maybe we'll beat your asses and let Jerry fuck the shit out of you, you fucking fags. You'd like that wouldn't you?"

Paul says:

"No. Not really." He turns and walks away through the crowd of people that have circled around us. The brothers of Delta Kappa Epsilon look at me. I think they've been completely shut down by the fact that Paul has handled this conflict in the way he has. It's like getting mugged and asking the mugger for the time: he doesn't know what to do, and it upsets the balance of power. I think I saw that on The Learning Channel as well, some show on psychology. Unfortunately, I don't believe there was a segment on what to do when your best friend leaves you with a horde of angry fraternity brothers.

"Well, go on with your boyfriend. Run."

I'm thankful they're releasing me peacefully. I don't think

my psyche could have withstood Jerry's bunny-like ferocity plundering my rectum. I shrug my shoulders and turn and walk off slowly. As I've said, I don't run for anything. It's unnatural.

We couldn't find Craig so Paul and I walked back to the house. In all honesty we didn't look very hard; sticking around seemed like an unwise decision, just in case Jerry and his posse got all hopped up on Molsons and decided to come looking for us again. We figured the girls were doing okay on their own.

Back at the house we've turned on the television to see what is shaking down. Our worst fears have been realized: it's all over. CNN is playing the tail end of a statement being made by the chief of police in which he commends the work of his dedicated officers, blah blah blah. Paul says:

"Well, what happened?" The news announcer, who looks as though he's about to crackup, says:

"Once again, recapping the events tonight in Syracuse, New York: a lone gunman, who is as of yet unidentified, drove his automobile through the front of a McDonald's, took hostages, and proceeded to force the employees to fill his car with Chicken McNuggets and Filets o'Fish. About three hours after seizing control of the restaurant he released the patrons, all of whom were unharmed except for minor injuries incurred when the alleged gunman's car entered the premises. The gunman released the hostages with bags of food for officers who had the building surrounded, and approximately two and a half hours later, when his car was filled with food, took his own life. We'll have more on this very bizarre and breaking—" Paul shuts the television off and slumps back on the couch. He takes out his cigarettes, hands one to me, takes one for himself, lights them both and says:

"Do you think that midget is fucking our women right now?"

"I've no idea. It might be a good thing for Megan. He might be just the right size."

"What do you make of all this? I mean, is the world just screwed up or what? It seems like there should have been something more to it all..." He trails off, exhaling rings of smoke.

I want to say something, but I don't know what to say. Paul is right, though: there seems like there should be something more. I don't know what that something should be, but I feel its absence. Maybe what I'm missing is the motivation. Kids shooting up a school or a church, I mean, you kind of get that. It doesn't make it any less twisted, but I could see where someone might have been dealt a bad hand by his or her classmates or youth leader and felt the need to exact some vengeance. It's rough dealing with hormones and acne for the first time. And then you throw the good looking kids into the mix whose families buy them a Mazda for their 16th birthday and whose skin is always crystal clear—it's a complete mystery to me why more people aren't unloading rounds in the streets everyday.

Paul says:

"Let's go for a ride, Jordan. Lourdene left her keys here."

"Where are we going?"

"Out of this one horse town, baby."

"Okay."

When I was in elementary school, and up until I was in high school, my dad was big on just taking drives. He always said we were going somewhere: the zoo, Green Lakes Park, the State Fair... just wherever. Sometimes we actually went where he said we were going, but more often than not we found ourselves someplace else.

Once we left to go to the movies and wound up at an apple orchard to get some fresh cider. Since it was the beginning of fall, dad had decided he'd like some hot cider before bed. It was early October and the leaves were starting to change. Kelly and I ran off through the orchard; I can't recall if we were chasing after one another or just glad to be out of the city and we didn't know what to do with all that open space. It was overcast that day, and it was like the colors of the leaves were reflected back from the clouds, and everything had an odd amber tint to it.

I got tired of running and I flopped under a tree and stared up through the branches. I don't remember thinking of anything. I just remember being really content. Not happy, and not what you might consider mellow, but just really at peace with everything. Maybe that's where I started the habit of just chilling out and thinking. I remember my mom and dad walked through the orchard with their arms wrapped around one another, and Kelly was chasing after them, and it never once occurred to me then that I would grow up and things would be any different. I had no concept of time or change, even right there, in the midst of all those trees slowly shedding their leaves like fading sparks. Eventually Kelly and I got to the point where we'd rather hang out with our friends than go on some lame drive with our parents, so it just became mom and dad, and it wasn't long after that mom got sick. I doubt they've been on a drive since then.

But to think that Paul and I would attempt grand theft auto with Lourdene's car and wing our way out of central New York is too much to hope for. This trip is no different than the ones my father took the family on when I was younger. We end up on the south end of Comstock, out at the entrance to the abandoned quarry where the athletes from the University go to jog. Paul parks the car and rolls the windows down, then he pulls out his bowl and lights it and we pass it back and forth until it's cashed. Paul says:

"We should just drive out of here, man. I mean out. Like somewhere else entirely. Like another state or something."

"I think that's illegal."

"Yeah. So is this."

"Yeah." We both laugh. I can feel myself getting a little sleepy. I don't know why; I slept most of the day. I say:

"Did you ever want to do something? Like, you know, something?"

"Like a job?"

"Yeah, okay."

Paul leans his head back and closes his eyes. I reach over and turn the ignition key slightly so we can listen to the radio. Lourdene has left a cassette in the tape deck and the first I thing I hear is Phish singing: *No left turn unstoned.* I think maybe I'm just high or something, but they sing it again, and I try to unravel its mystery. Then I remember I asked Paul a question and he hasn't answered. I can't remember how long ago I asked him, so I wait.

I can't remember how long I've been waiting so I say:

"Dude. You fall asleep?"

"No."

"Well, what is it then?"

"I don't know. I've been sitting here thinking about it, but I can't remember ever wanting to do anything. I've never had a job. No one ever made me get one. No one ever asked me what I wanted to do. I mean, even in school, you know, with all that math and shit they told me I'd use later on, no one ever asked me what I wanted to use it for. Didn't we have a guidance counselor or something? Is that just some urban legend or something? Are there really guidance counselors and was I given the shaft in high school or what?"

"Yeah man, there really are guidance counselors. But I didn't see one either. I think they only put their efforts towards kids going to college or pregnant chicks. We didn't show up on their radar."

"Well that absolutely sucks dude. I want some guidance. I want answers. I want out. Who was the guidance counselor at our school?"

"I couldn't even begin to tell you."

Paul leans forward and looks very pained as though it is an effort for him to enunciate clearly.

"I think we should find out and track this person down and lodge a complaint with them or the powers that be. We should register the sorry state of affairs we find ourselves in, stuck in this town without prospects of leaving—or living."

"Isn't that the same state of affairs the powers that be are in? I mean, if they're here, they seem pretty stuck too."

"Quite so, old sport." Paul starts to giggle. His eyes are half open. "At the very least I think we are owed two bus tickets and a map."

"You can buy the two bus tickets right now."

Paul shifts in the seat and sighs.

"Yeah, but that would require some effort on my part, and as lousy as this place is, I just figure we'd end up somewhere equally lousy, with other people who think where they live sucks, and that the grass is greener elsewhere. I just don't feel like putting in the effort to find out I'm right. Or wrong for that matter. I mean, you know, I'd rather be somewhere else, but I get by here, and I know a lot of people who aren't even doing that, so it's all good I guess."

My head feels heavy, tranquil. It seems like forever since Paul finished talking. The clock on the dash board hasn't changed. Is it even working? I can't tell. I haven't been paying attention. I focus on it now. Nothing is happening. I look out the window at the city twinkling a few miles from us. It seems empty and unreal. Everything feels that way, like a false backdrop to my life that sleeps whenever I am away from it. Maybe I'm dreaming.

"Did I tell you about the dream I had the other night?" Paul isn't even looking at me, and I wonder if he's really asked it.

"Are you reading my thoughts?"

"You're high."

I put my head back, then lean forward and shake it, as if that will clear out the cobwebs. I lean back again. Paul says:

"I used to have this poster above my bed. It was the size of an average bedroom door and it was a picture of that door in the opening sequence of the *Twilight Zone*. You know what I'm talking about?"

I don't say anything.

"Dude, you know what I'm talking about?"

"Yeah." I feel like I'm swimming upside down and dizzy.

"Anyway, I had this dream one time that there were naked women on the other side of the door, and I woke up standing in my bed clawing at the door. It was messed up."

"That is messed up."

"That's not the worst. I mean, I've always been a half-assed sleep walker. I don't really walk anywhere. I just wake up doing something twisted. So the other night I dream my dick is really this big bouquet of candy canes, and I'm saying to Lourdene in my dream, *Don't you want a candy cane? Who doesn't love a candy cane?* I wake up and I'm shoving my wang in her mouth and she's all freaked out cause she was asleep and it was like I was raping her or something. She got up and ran out of the room. It was whack."

"What did you do?"

"I went back to sleep."

I nod and look down at Syracuse glimmering below us and trying to make sense of the day. I feel like I'm coming up for air.

"Do you have any more weed?"

"Back at the place."

"Well, what are we doing here?"

"Well spoken my boy." Paul fires up the car, puts it into gear, then turns to me:

"What did you want to be?"

"What?"

"In school. What did you want to be?"

"I think I just wanted to be happy."

"That's about the gayest shit I've ever heard. Get out. You're walking home because that's some seriously gay shit."

"What I meant was happy, you know, while banging three chicks at the same time and wearing one of those hats that holds two beer cans with straws coming out of them and into your mouth."

"That's better. Disturbing, but somehow still better."

CHAPTER FIVE

Like Any Other Day

I AM AWAKENED BY A leg cramp that jolts me out of a dark slumber. I am surprised—but only briefly—that I am in my own bed for a change. And then it comes back to me.

The girls never showed up at Paul's place, never called, and eventually Paul passed out and I got tired of waiting. I don't know why I just didn't crash there, but for some reason I felt suddenly like being outside despite the fact that I was sleepy. It had cooled down a lot, but the humidity was still miserable. I didn't ride my board home either; I walked. Which is why, I suspect, that I have been stricken with a cramp. I'm not used to hoofing it so much. You'd think that the board would keep the legs in shape, but you'd be wrong. I don't try to work it like I did when I was in high school, with all that acrobatic nonsense. I got tired of the scrapes and slamming my testicles against fixed objects. It's strictly for transport now.

I didn't walk straight home; I took the scenic route, so to speak, wandering through some of the nicer neighborhoods on the east side of Westcott Street. Nicer in the sense that people make an attempt at trimming the hedges and the small plot of grass they call a lawn. All of the houses were dark, and I wondered if everyone was just exhausted from being on edge all night with anticipation about what was happening at the McDonald's, or if they just didn't care. In fact, I was having a hard time deciding whether or not I cared. I feel like I used to get worked up about things a lot more. These days I find myself accepting of everything that comes my way with a casual indifference. If I thought getting worked up would do any good, I don't know, maybe I'd show a little enthusiasm. But what's to get enthused about? The next step in my life appears to be getting a job and busting my balls and moving out of parents' house. And then the continued busting of my balls to stay out. Where's the excitement in that? Not that I'm opposed to work, but I see my dad doing something that he hates, day after day, and he doesn't seem too happy. What's worse is that he doesn't seem to stop and question it—he just accepts the fact that his life is supposed to be miserable. It's not just him. I see plenty of people working stupid little jobs and they're so bitter about it. And I don't guess there's any way to avoid it, because if it could be done, don't you think all those people would be doing it? Which is the conclusion I arrived at last night: sure, I care about a guy shooting up the McDonald's, and the freakish way that he did it, but I only care because it takes my mind off the fact that life is a pretty dismal arrangement and it's only going to get more bleak. It distracts me for a little while anyway.

I don't know what I was doing over there on Allen Street and

Fellows Avenue. Or I do. It wouldn't be the first time I had walked along those tree lined blocks, looking at houses bigger and better than what I could ever hope to obtain. I sometimes wonder if mom and dad, on one of their drives without me and Kelly, cruised through these neighborhoods and thought of what they might have had, had they not been saddled with kids, and then the monster portion of mom's doctor bills that the insurance wouldn't cover.

I walk down the hall and into the kitchen. Dad has two grapefruit halves on his plate: he has scooped one down to its shell, and he is slicing into the next one with delicacy. He doesn't look at me when he says:

"How about it, huh?"

"What's that?"

"All that shooting yesterday. Why didn't you wake me?"

"You were sleeping."

"Well, I guess you were trying to think anyway. What do you make of it?"

"Pretty weird." I open the refrigerator and take out a Coke. I feel like I might go on a little quest for another poster and come back later and take a nap. I like sleeping in the afternoon; my dreams are really vivid.

"Weird? Here." He slides the paper to the edge of the kitchen table. I sit down with my Coke and start to read. The facts are this:

The shooter's name was Dean Peterson. He worked as a DJ at a topless bar called Xanadu's. He was not married, had no family, and no history of mental illness. However, the district attorney said that had he not gone bonkers and shot himself, they were about a week away from charging him with twenty counts of felonious kidnapping of livestock. There is no mention of what he did with the livestock, only that it was in relation to another pending case. Also, Dean Peterson had a serious addiction to cough syrup. The article described his apartment was littered with empty bottles, and while the autopsy hasn't come back yet, there's no doubt in the Police Chief's mind that Peterson's blood will be soaked with the stuff.

Jesus. Some people. Dad tries again:

"So how about it?"

"That cough syrup. It's deadly."

"You laugh but this is the next great threat to American Youth. You can read about it inside on one of those other pages. There's a whole story on the dangers of drinking a whole bottle of plain old cough syrup, just like the kind you can buy at any store. The head of the DEA in New York says it poses a greater threat to the youth of America now than crack. There are a lot of sick kids in this country today, and they're desperate to destroy themselves. There's something terribly wrong with this country when kids are killing one another, killing their parents, getting high on cough syrup. What is wrong with your generation, Jordan? I just don't get it."

Apparently, my dad, hip guy of the street that he is, is aware of a trend in the recreational consumption of cough syrup that I am not. I look at the story on Dean Peterson again.

"Says here that this guy was 32."

"And that's just the kind of trash influencing children today.

A grown man like that ought to have a job, a house, and should be behaving like a responsible adult."

I want to ask my dad how Dean Peterson was able to influence children by working at a topless club, but I'm not in the mood to listen to his rationale. I stand up from the table and start back to my room.

"Jordan?"

"Yes?"

"Don't you go back to bed. I tried to do as best as I could with you and your sister, and I've failed. If I had done a good job you'd be out looking for work right now. Five places. You understand? I want you applying at five places today."

I love these guilt trips. They are, most likely, why I look so guilty all the time. After twenty years of being told I've done something wrong, how could I look otherwise?

"That's what I was planning on, dad."

"You're damn right you were."

Crouse Avenue showed no signs of having been the site of a major frenzy last night with the exception of some police barricades in front of the McDonald's. The people on Marshall street, the college kids and hospital employees, seemed as self-involved as usual. I might have been a little more curious about the whole crime scene myself but I was on a crusade.

And very much like The Crusades my own was a complete failure. I love The Learning Channel for that: it gives me standards in history to which I can flimsily compare my own meager efforts.

I looked through the posters at the record store on Adams

Street, Oliver's. I'm in there every couple of weeks, seeing if they have anything new, and by now I should know better. I go to the Flag Lady, a shop on Marshall Street, but most of their posters are those magic eye things, or ridiculous fantasy art with titles like *Virtual Infinity*, geared towards stoned frat boys who want to be deep and stare at computer generated images when they're high. Which I'm down with, but please, *Virtual Infinity?* What a ludicrous phrase.

I'm beginning to think I'm never going to get my room exactly the way I like it. It pisses me off. I mean, Christ, it's just a poster. You'd think it'd be easier than it is. Then I remind myself of the *G.I. Joe* comic and of the Zen Master: 30 years. I'm not even close to approaching that. If I find a poster in my allotted time frame of a year I will have achieved some sort of enlightenment in record time. Yo Joe.

A T-shirt shop has a sign in the window: Help Wanted. I pause briefly then continue walking.

I duck into No Borders No Boundaries for a cup of coffee. Waking up so early has me dragging. This big hippie behind the counter stubs out his cigarette and raises his eyebrows at me.

I take my coffee and go sit down on a couch over by a window to catch the breeze. This place is on the second floor above J. Michael's Shoes and with it being so hot lately it's terribly uncomfortable. In hindsight I should have gotten an iced coffee. I'm really bummed now. I only had money for one or the other, and I don't think I can enjoy a regular cup of coffee now. I hate the way the cosmos confounds me sometimes.

I look across at the girl sitting on the couch opposite me.

It's her.

Without her teal polo work shirt she looks completely different. She's wearing a black tank top with spaghetti straps that exposes her middle: she has a navel ring. Even though it's hot she's wearing jeans. I love seeing legs, but there's something I love about a girl in jeans. It's the denim. It's sexy. It has to be one of the five sexiest fabrics known to man.

I don't think she knows it's me, the guy who plundered the plumbing at her place of work. She looks up at me and smiles, then looks back down at the book she's reading.

She brushes some of those red locks behind her ear. I feel a warmth spreading out from inside me. I am filled with the urge to petition some king or queen of a small country for a capital investment so that I may lead a band of merry men and scoundrels on adventures to new lands that I will conquer in the name of this girl. But, alas, what new lands are left to conquer?

I am suddenly very awake. I want to put some Nirvana on a stereo somewhere and rage. I have the hankering for a good old fashioned mosh pit. I think everyone in here should know my name. I want to create a spectacle. I want that center of the world thing to be true. Seriously. This is how I feel, and I know it's the most ridiculous thing, but seeing her brush that strand of hair behind her ear: it feels like something I'll never forget, like an assassination. Aren't there images permanently ingrained in everyone's memory but on a personal level? I'm not thinking about the napalm girl photo, or the Challenger exploding, or even a Pinto sticking out through the front of a

McDonald's, but something that only you glimpsed?

I wish I knew a way to explain how her fingers delicately pushing her hair behind her ear has struck me so completely.

I'm suddenly reminded of the last time my family went to my grandmother's house on Lake Ontario. I was fourteen, about to be fifteen. It was the morning before we left. I had gone out walking along the shore. Hardly anyone else was out there. It was a Monday, and dad wasn't working until the next night so we were able to stay for an extra day. When I got down to the beach there was a girl who had just come in from a swim, and she was standing there with the water lapping against her knees, and she was wringing her hair out, the sun shimmering across the water. It was like a movie. I felt then just like I do now: electric. I want to shed my cool composure and declare, *Golly gee whiz you're pretty*. Fortunately, I have a safety mechanism that prevents these little outbursts.

Lia is wearing a hemp necklace with what appears to be military dog tags on them. I don't know what to make of that. If her dad is in the army, then I don't think she's going to want anything to do with me. Still, I figure this is my opening. I mean, it's better than, *Hey, did the toilet start working again?* I ask:

"Are those dog tags?"

She looks up at me, raises her eyebrows.

"What? Oh. Yeah, actually. My dog Mitzy. She got hit by a car a few years ago."

"Oh. I thought they were military dog tags."

"No, no. Just tags from my dog."

"So your dog wasn't in the military?"

She laughs a little. I laugh a little. I say:

"I never had a dog. My parents wouldn't let me."

"That's so sad."

"Well, not really now that I think about it. I don't think I would have been too good at taking care of it. I haven't quite figured out how to take of myself yet." She laughs a little again. I smile. "I figure until I can take care of myself I shouldn't ruin the life of another living creature."

"Good boy." I can feel myself turning to butter. There's something about those words…

"So what are you reading?"

"It's a book about babies. Their brains. It's hard to explain."

"Huh."

"It's just something that interests me." She looks down at her book, blushes a little. "You look really familiar. Did we go to school together?"

A voice in the back of my head urges, *Say yes. Say yes. Do not admit where you know her from. Danger Will Robinson! Danger!* But I'm a terrible liar. How could I ever be expected to be effective at masking the truth when for no reason I often assume a look of absolute criminality? It's a horrible curse: I am forever forced to tell the truth because my face will betray me every time if I dare speak otherwise. I see Lia's face go dark.

"Wait. No fucking way," Lia says.

"What?"

"You're the retard from yesterday."

"What? What are you talking about? We went to school together. I think we had trigonometry together. Wasn't it trig?"

She rolls her eyes and closes her book. It was worth a shot anyway.

"I never took trig, and you are *definitely* the guy who tried to slink out after stopping up the toilet yesterday and the whole back of the store stunk for hours."

She's talking kind of loud, and I look away from her and around the shop. People have looked up from their coffee and their chess games to see what this is all about. This isn't what I had in mind when I said I wanted to make a spectacle.

"Look, about that. I'm really sorry."

She lets out a breath.

"Yeah."

"No, really, I am. I behaved badly. I'm sorry. I took care of it didn't I? I'm sorry. I wanted to say that yesterday, but... Look, just— I'm sorry."

She looks up at the ceiling, then back at me.

"Okay."

"Okay."

We stare at each other. I look down at my coffee. I look back up at her. She looks down at her book. Then she looks back up at me:

"Okay. So what do you want?"

"I was thinking maybe we could like, you know, talk or something."

"So talk."

I hate it when people get like this. Because what do you say? If I start chatting like nothing has happened she's going to think I'm a complete idiot. If I try and apologize again I'll look desperate. If I don't say anything I admit defeat. Actually, I think defeat is fairly imminent no matter what I do. Story of my life.

"So do you have a boyfriend?"

"I have to go." She stands and grabs a backpack that was sitting on the floor next to her. I scramble for the save:

"Are you a student?"

"No."

So much for that. I stand up too. I don't know why.

"Well, maybe I'll see you around sometime."

"Seems unlikely. But have a nice life anyway." She turns and starts off. I say:

"Hey." Lia stops and turns and gives me a look. "Why does that seem unlikely?"

She takes a step forward.

"Look, just because I've had the misfortune of crossing paths with you twice in two days does not mean my life is on such a downward spiral that it will happen again. So why don't we just savor the memories of these two chance encounters and try not to ruin what we've shared already. Okay?"

She doesn't give me the opportunity to even stammer out a response. She turns and walks off briskly. A guy at a nearby table who has witnessed this train wreck of interaction says:

"Jesus, dude, that was a serious shutdown she just gave you. What did you do? Piss on her floor?"

"Close."

CHAPTER SIX

In Terms of Two

PAUL AND I ARE SITTING on his back porch drinking beers, not saying much of anything. My stomach churns. After my miserable failure at talking to A-Plus Girl at No Borders yesterday I was in a serious funk. Paul was in a serious funk because once again we had nowhere to go. I reminded him of our conversation the previous night in which he had declared he didn't really want to go anywhere. Paul said to me:

"I spoke with hard words last night man, and it went against everything I've ever said." I'm not sure what he meant by that. He can be real dramatic when he's down.

To combat our mutual sullenness we decided to see what this cough medicine business was all about. We went to three different drug stores; the first two wouldn't sell us any. Apparently the local news had been doing special spots along the lines of *Protect Your Children: Death by Decongestant*.

We each bought an eight-ounce bottle and turned them up.

Within an hour we were deathly nauseous and spent the rest

of the night lying around and feeling mildly delirious. It was far from pleasurable. The Colombian drug cartels will sleep easier, I'm sure. I've been feeling queasy off and on all day, and my bowels have spoken to me of their displeasure on numerous occasions. My nose feels like the Sahara and all day long I've been chugging water. If I had spent years doing this to myself I would have taken out a fast food place, too.

I can hear the girls inside talking about some guys they met the other night while they were putting Megan back together at the Tri-Delt house. Which didn't take much effort; there wasn't a scratch on her: she was merely stunned. A wayward Frisbee can do that, I guess. Lara is saying:

"So he's studying retail management. Can you believe that? I mean, if *I* was going to study something, that would be like right at the top of *my* list."

Paul and I share a look. I say:

"Retail Management? What is that?"

"You learn to manage I guess."

From inside I catch:

"And so then he just blows on it, and at first it kind of tickled, but for some reason it felt so good after that."

"I hope to God she's not talking about the midget," Paul says.

"As if I don't have enough reasons to end my life."

"Cough syrup still got you down?"

"Not so much. But yeah. A little. I mean, I feel a lot better today, dude, but I'm just bummed. It's like I was saying yesterday, there's this girl—"

"Whoa, champ. Hold on a sec."

Paul gets up and goes inside. I hear the stereo start throwing out some Sleater-Kinney. He comes back out with two more beers and says:

"No need to risk a riot. If the girls heard you say that they'd be on the phone to Megan in a second and our happy little world would come crashing down around us. Now, pray tell, what about this girl?"

I take a cigarette from Paul's pack laying on the table between us.

"I told you about her. A-Plus girl. At the gas station."

"Right, right. Sorry, dude. I wasn't paying much attention yesterday. I was just holding it together trying not to yak cough medicine all over the place."

"It's all considered." I take a long drag on the cigarette. My stomach gurgles at me. "I told you about yesterday, at No Borders, and the day before when I clogged the toilet—"

"I remember that part."

"—but it's more than that." I stop and put out my cigarette. If I try to smoke the whole thing I'm going to make myself sick. "I'm having a hard time explaining myself, man. This girl... I don't know thing one about her, right? All I know is her name and that she pretty much seems content to avoid me. But when she looks at me—and not in the menacing way that has constituted most of our eye contact—but really looks at me, and the sound of her voice... I don't know what it is. It's like, too much. It hurts. That's the only way I know to say it. It hurts."

I look at Paul. He is staring at me.

"Jesus, dude."

I nod.

"How much of that foul, generic cough concoction did you drink? You're talking some crazy moon man language."

"Shut the fuck up."

"No, seriously, this is madness."

I don't respond. Instead, I examine my beer, and slowly start peeling the label off.

"What about Megan?"

"You know how I feel about that."

"Look, I know she's been making it tough on you lately..."

"Dude, she's giving me an ulcer. Sex is not supposed to give you an ulcer."

Paul nods his head.

"But you were *the guy*. You went in there first. All others before you failed. Your kung-fu was superior. Don't you at least owe her some time?"

"But that's just it: my kung-fu wasn't superior. If it was I'd be getting laid like a porn star every day, all day. I have failed, and I have failed in the worst way: I can't close the deal."

Paul appears to ponder this.

"All right, man, I'm behind you. Whatever you want to do. Fuck it."

Paul holds up his beer to me. I raise mine and clink it against his and turn it up.

"Sometimes I wish I could get a stand-in, someone to do what I can't with Megan, then lets me take over."

"You want me to bang your girlfriend? I'll get on that right now and tear it up, man. I'll grab her hair and slap her ass and make her call me Tonto." Craig appears beside me, thrusting his hips forward and making a motion as though he were slapping some imaginary woman's butt.

"How long have you been standing there?" Paul says.

"Long enough to hear that Jordan needs someone to bat cleanup."

"Craig," I say, "first of all, batting cleanup means you're fourth in line. Secondly, why did you ever move back here?"

He stops gyrating his pelvis next to my head and crosses his arms.

"I don't know. It just seems you have to work everywhere else. The parents are here, I've got my old room, rent free, no bills, just getting by. And I've got my buds!" He dives across me onto Paul and wrestles him to the ground, flipping Paul onto his stomach and play-humping him from behind. "You ready to go to Chuck's, bitch?"

Paul, very calmly, says:

"Not like this." Craig hops up.

"Okay then, let's go."

Chuck's is an underground bar in the most literal sense. It's a Syracuse institution. There's no windows, and thus no ventilation, so there's this awful funk about the place that seeps into your clothes and hair and it stays with you until you wash it out. Other than that it's an all right place to go if you don't mind paying a dollar for a game of pool and having a choice between piss poor beer and Boone's Farm.

When we make the turn in front of Bruegger's Bagels to cut down the alley to Chuck's no one pays the slightest bit of attention to the yellow police tape that has been wrapped around the McDonald's. I want to stop and look, thinking I might see something, you know, but I don't know what it is that I want to see. Besides, the police have been sweeping over things for two days and I figure they've carted off anything remotely interesting.

I get stamped underage like I do every time. We all do, except for Lourdene, because she has a fake ID. On top of this humiliation we have to pay a full cover for the band because we are (allegedly) not drinking. I'll be glad when I turn 21 in December so I can start going across the street to Faegan's where they have 36 beers on tap and all the women own cars.

Craig and Paul and I grab a booth near the pool table while Lourdene goes and orders a few pitchers of Molson. Brenda and Lara go off to talk to some guys that look like frat types. I suspect they are the ones they met the other night while being held captive in the Tri-Delt house. I'm looking at all the fraternity letters carved into the table top when Paul says:

"Hey, check it."

I look up at him and he's staring across the bar at these three girls at another table. The two facing me are pretty good looking. One of them has big hair, but I find that kind of attractive these days on a woman. It's retro, you know, like platforms and bell-bottoms. The girl with her back to me takes a cigarette away from her mouth, and there's something about the way she does it, and the shirt she's wearing is cut so her shoulders are exposed, and I can't help but just gawk at the slope of them. She turns around and looks dead at me, but really more like right through me, and it's Lia.

"She's checking me out," Craig says.

"That's her man. That's totally her."

"What?"

"That's A-Plus Girl. The girl who gave me a plunger." Craig says:

"I'd like to give her my plunger if you know what I mean."

Paul stares blankly at Craig for a second then looks at me:

"So that's her?"

"Yeah."

"I can't see her face that well. I'm going to get some change for the cigarette machine and do a fly-by." Paul stands and walks over toward the table where Lia and her friends are sitting and gives them all the most blatant look. I watch him get some change, not buy cigarettes, and then pass by their table again with the big fish eye. One of the girls (not Lia) says something to him. He stops and starts talking, points over at our booth. The girls look over. I lean back. Craig says:

"Fuck yeah, motherfucker." Then: "Who is this A-Plus girl?"

"Shut the fuck up."

I try to play it cool again, take a cigarette from Craig's pack of GPC's laying on the table, light it. Craig says:

"Are we in?" Paul says:

"Are you some kind of idiot? My girlfriend is here. His girlfriend will show up here. Even if we were in we wouldn't be in because our girls are here to keep us out."

"So what did they want?" I'm hoping it was something about me. It has to be.

"They wanted to know if I had a lighter; I left mine at the table."

"Oh, that wasn't about a lighter," Craig says. "That was about the dick."

"Dude, you think everything is about the dick. It's not. Sometimes people just need a lighter. Now if they were going to smoke your dick, then asking me for a lighter would be about dick."

Craig isn't even paying attention to Paul. He's looking past him and he says:

"Hey, Jordan man, that chick is checking you out."

She is. Just sitting there, smoking her cigarette, placing it against her lips and taking these long deep drags, the smoke seeming to melt right out of her mouth. Paul says:

"I think you need to make your move now, fat cat."

"Dude, this girl has witnessed me trying to skip out after stopping up the toilet in her workplace. She didn't want anything to do with me then, she didn't want anything to do with me yesterday when my bowels were acting properly, and she sure doesn't want anything to do with me now. And what about the girls?"

"I'll cover. Go over there and try and make some sort of recovery. You've got nowhere to go but up."

I can't deny the truth of this. However, I have a boner. I don't want to wait for it to go away because doing that is the opposite of trying to get a boner when you're completely limp: when it's hard and you need it otherwise it stays absurdly stiff. I slide out of the booth and as I stand I do a little twist and run my hands down the front of my shorts like I'm straightening them out, but if you took a look at me you'd know the last thing I care about is wrinkle free shorts. I get my wang in a better place, but the way it's running down my leg I'm afraid if I get too excited, or if I laugh, it'll flex and blatantly bang against my shorts leg and make them tent out and everyone will know I'm sporting a boner in my pocket. A-Plus girl is still just giving me this look, so I take a drag off of my cigarette then go to put it out. But I don't know what I'll do with my hands, so I pause and don't put it out, but I realize how stupid this must look so I look at my cigarette thoughtfully like I just noticed there's a little more to smoke. I give it another drag and put it out and when glance up A-Plus girl is still looking at me.

"Would you just go the fuck over there."

Paul gives me a little shove, which makes me feel like a complete tool, but I am moving forward now. Inertia is on my side. She can't be more than twenty feet off, but it feels like I'm in one of those dreams where you're running down a hallway and no matter how fast you run you just can't seem to get to the end. Of course, I've never had a dream like that, and I don't know anyone who has, but people in horror films seem to frequently have dreams to that effect so someone must have them.

This whole time we're just staring at each other, like right dead on into each other's eyes. She takes a deep, seductive drag off of her cigarette, and I'm walking forward, trying not to do anything stupid with my hands. I put them in my pockets to get them out of them way, and also to cover my bone which is starting to pulsate. I mean this chick just does something to me.

Paul and I watched this show on The Learning Channel one time that was about mating. It gave the run down on how all sorts of different species mate, how they select a partner, the whole biology of it. When it got to humans the narrator began talking about how we think we're so different from the rest of the animal kingdom, when in reality we're not. We still look for healthy mates and we still have our little rituals (like this crossing of the bar thing I'm doing right now). Anyway, one of the points this show made was that sometimes we're just wicked attracted to people without explanation for the simple reason of chemicals, pheromones and other variables we can't control. It seems believable, especially right now, because just looking at this girl rocks my nuts. Which, I realize, lacks the eloquence of how she makes my soul burn, but cut me some slack—I've had a few beers already tonight. And you know, I'd almost swear I could hear her saying my name, like in some weird telepathic way, as if she's commanding me over to her.

Someone grabs me and spins me around. It's Megan. She says:

"Hey! Why didn't you call me today?"

I look over my shoulder at Lia but she's turned her back to me. A voice comes over the PA system: *Put your hands together for SkaCago!* The band cranks into an up-tempo ska version of "You're the Inspiration." Megan is saying something but I can't hear her over the horns. I look at Paul and he is shaking his head. I feel suddenly very bitter toward the world.

I'm leaned back on the couch in Paul's apartment. He passes me a bowl, I take a quick puff, then pass it over to Megan who takes a deep drag, holds the smoke in, and passes it over to Craig. We've got the lights down low and some unplugged Nirvana crooning on the stereo. Chuck's was pretty beat: it didn't seem like there was a scene happening (I guess because people might think the place is still closed from the action the other day), and you can only listen to a ska Chicago cover band for so long before you want to start mutilating yourself in some attempt to get the noise out of your head.

Megan is curled against me and she keeps trying to kiss me every so often. She gets extremely amorous when she smokes, and I know that if we were alone right about now I'd be falling into the trap that I am so accustomed to: that she is ready, willing, and able. She is at least the first two. I'm trying to find an excuse to stay here for the night and not walk her home where I will inevitably end up on the couch in her parents' basement, attempting to ease my smaller self into her with all the care of someone diffusing a bomb. Lara says:

"I can't wait to get the fuck out of here."

Nobody says anything. Then Brenda says:

"Tired? Head home?"

Paul tells her to leave his place if she doesn't like it, and she clarifies:

"No, not here, but *here*. This whole place is a drag. I'm going to go down to my dad's in Queens and live with him for a while. So I don't have to sit around with my finger in my ass all day."

"What are you going to do in Queens?" I ask.

"What am I *not* going to do in Queens. Haven't you ever been to the city? It never stops. Lisa says—" Craig cuts in:

"Who's Lisa?"

"One of the girls from the house," Brenda explains.

"What house?"

"Tri-Delt."

"How do you know girls from Tri-Delt?" Craig seems genuinely confused.

"Jesus, dude. Where the fuck is your head? You were there." Paul takes a cigarette out of his pack and can't quite get it lit. He takes the cigarette out of his mouth and shakes it at Craig. "You see how pissed off you make me sometimes?"

"I just want to know who these sorority girls are, and why they aren't here, doing a little Delta Delta Delta on my cocka cocka cocka."

Often, Craig serves as a reminder to us all that our high school diplomas aren't worth the paper they're printed on because he holds one as well. I inquire:

"So what did Lisa say?"

"Lisa says that if I live in Queens she could probably get me a job working at one of the boutiques her mother owns."

"Doing what?" Paul asks, not entirely with interest.

"Sales associate responsibilities."

"Do you have any experience at being a sales associate?"

"It's what I've always wanted to do."

"I thought you wanted to marry rich?" Craig says.

"A girl has to have some skills. Besides, my skills assessment test in school—"

"Wait: skills assessment? Did you meet with a guidance counselor?" Paul looks incredulous.

"Yes. At one point I was thinking of culinary school."

"Fuck!" I sense a rant coming on, but I've already heard it. I lean my head back against the couch...

Now that I think about it I never have been down to New

York, which is weird because I only live five hours away. You would think that on one of his directionless drives my dad would have carted the family in that vicinity. I'm trying to think of where I have been that's really far away, but my head feels so heavy.

Lara and the girls aren't listening to Paul go on about the guidance counselor, leaving him to yell at Craig about it. Megan is leaning against my shoulder, listening to Lara go on about what her dad's place is near, and how she would have this whole world within walking distance. I want to tell her that she has that now, but sometimes she can be a real piece of work, really a snob, so I don't speak to her, just keep my head leaned back, feeling Megan's arms curled around my right arm, and Kurt Cobain is singing softly about where the bad folks go when they die, and I have this rising and floating sensation in my body. It's like the place I have been that's kind of far away from here, my grandmother's house out at Lake Ontario, and when you've just gone past the point in the lake where your feet touch and the water has you bobbing up and down with the waves and everything. Mom and dad would be on the shore lying in the sun, and Kelly, she'd be in the water with me, and I'd dunk her, or we'd be trying to splash each other. Once we built a sand castle. Not a good one, but it's the only one I've ever built, just like in the movies, brother and sister on the beach building the Goddamned American Dream right there in the sand with mom and dad looking on— might as well have had Old Glory behind us flapping in the breeze coming off the lake. Then Kelly got older and she wouldn't come in the water anymore. She would just lie there in the sun with her shades on, not turning her head when guys walked past her and looked her up and down. I'd be out in the water just floating and nobody saying anything to me or looking at me, but I loved it because my grandmother's house was right there on the shore and it felt great not hearing police sirens all night or your neighbors fighting, or smelling the asphalt in your head like you do sometimes when it's so hot in the city during the summer. But, like everything else, we haven't been back in years. Not since mom's operation, because dad says she doesn't want to be out in public like that; she's afraid people would know what was wrong with her and she'd be embarrassed. Sometimes I think it's more dad who would be embarrassed.

I feel like I'm in the lake though, and my body feels kind of warm, like the sun is gently baking it, and someone is calling my name from the shore. Then Megan shakes me:

"Jordan?"

"Huh?" I must have drifted off, because it's just me and Megan on the couch, and the music has been turned off. The lava lamp is squeezing out a dim glow.

"Are you staying here?"

"Yeah, I'm feeling too buzzed to go home, or really to walk anywhere. Have all the girls left? I guess you need one of them to walk home with you, or give you a ride."

"No, I told my mom I was staying with Lourdene so I could stay with you. Paul brought us a blanket and a pillow."

Great. I lay my head back and stare up at the ceiling. This is just what I need. Megan stands up and starts peeling off her clothing, down to her bra and underwear. She looks at me:

"Aren't you going to get undressed?"

"I'm comfortable." I want to avoid intimacy as much as possible.

"Well, at least take off your shoes."

I kick my shoes off and then reach down and slip off my socks. Megan hops on the couch with me and immediately starts kissing my neck and ears. She thrusts her hand in my crotch and starts rubbing vigorously.

"Meg, I'm a little beat here."

"Oh, come on. I'm so horny right now."

Admittedly, I'm getting hard. But this is a bad idea. She's going to want to try and do it, and I really don't want to mess with the consequences right now. I can't believe I'm saying this. I'm still in my sexual prime, and this girl is throwing herself at me, and I am denying her. My life sucks. I take my hand and squeeze her breasts anyway.

"That's more like it."

I kiss her, and she kisses me back, and she's a little overly excited about it. I feel like she's about to choke me with her tongue. She pulls back and says:

"I'm already wet. Feel."

She takes my hand and pushes it down the front of her underwear. I say:

"Meg, I'm really tired."

"But I want you."

"That's fine, but I'm going to sleep." I pull away and turn my back to her, cross my arms over my chest and pull the blanket over me a little more. Normally I'd be incredibly uncomfortable because this couch is so small—my feet drape over one side and I am not an especially tall guy. But I'm coming down from this buzz and I feel like sinking into the cushions. Megan grabs my balls and gives them a little squeeze.

"Come on, Jordan—don't quit on me."

"Look. Cut it out."

She doesn't say anything, and suddenly I feel like a total bastard. I roll back toward her and open my eyes. I can see her face lit somewhat by the lava lamp. She's on her back, staring up at the ceiling. She is a very pretty girl, with the sweetest face. It was Paul that set us up. I knew her already from just hanging out, but she was just some girl that came around and occasionally we talked. But Paul told her one day that she was going out with me on a date because I needed it. I wasn't really that keen on the idea, and I don't think she was either. We went and saw a movie at the Westcott Cinema—some foreign film because I thought it would be very cool to take a chick to see a movie with subtitles. It drove me nuts.

Afterwards, we got a few slices at Dorian's, then walked over into Oakwood Cemetery. It's this massive graveyard along Comstock Avenue, and it's filled with all these old mausoleums. It even has a pyramid in which a Mason is buried —real Illuminati weirdness. There's always a bunch of people smoking herb or drinking in the shadowy corners that border the university.

We went walking back where it was so dark you couldn't see your hands in front of your face, and just talked. I mean, I guess it was really no different than the thousands of dates that other people have everyday: we talked about our families, what we liked and what we didn't. And she made me laugh. And I made her laugh, and that was really the best part. This is all so sappy to think about, but it's really what happened. I think that's all you can hope for sometimes in this life: just someone to laugh at your jokes. I think I picked that from some bullshit Hallmark movie. But it's true. What they never tell you in those feel-good movies is that having someone who makes you laugh is all well and good until they start complaining about your penis tearing them up.

"I'm sorry." When she doesn't say anything I roll back into my position, snuggle into the blanket—Paul has the air conditioner cranked like he's Mr. Freeze—and feel myself getting sucked into sleep.

"It's okay. I still love you. You know that, don't you?"

I know I'm on the couch, lying next to Megan, but for a split second I think I'm in my bed at home, and A-Plus girl, Lia, is there beside me. I can feel her body pressed against mine, so close, and she is nude, like I can just roll over and kiss her, feel the soft skin of her shoulders as my lips press against them, whisper her name as I begin to pull her body closer to mine.

"What?"

I feel Megan pull back from me, and I'm not sure what's going on, or where I am, but it happens so quickly it's really not worth mentioning because I know what I've done so I say:

"You know, oui—French for yes. Yes I know you still love me. Oui."

"Oh." She presses against me. I think she says something else, but everything is fading.

CHAPTER SEVEN

Chivalry (Otherwise Known as Stalking)

I HEAR CARS PASSING ALONG the street and workmen doing road repairs, which seems to be a constant in Syracuse during the summer since the winter weather is so harsh on the pavement. Megan is still asleep, her body spooned against mine, and my crotch feels very sweaty. I carefully lift myself up off the couch, and when I pull back the covers this rank smell comes wafting out. I must have been leaking the cheap beer bubbles all night. I'm glad Megan is asleep for this. I put my shoes and socks back on. Megan stirs a little but she doesn't wake up. She's a heavy sleeper and I'm grateful for that. I just want to split.

It's humid again this morning, but there's a light breeze blowing, and when I slap my deck down on the pavement and start kicking it the wind kind of makes it all bearable. I cruise past all the houses looming with their weight and size along the uneven street, warped from all those winters and oak roots gnarling under the asphalt. There's hardly any small houses in Syracuse: everything is massive, like the mausoleums, monuments to better times when sprawling families were harbored in stately dwellings. But this is a dirty little town now. I'm glad it snows here six to nine months out of the year so that it at least looks pure and good half the time.

I feel my stomach start rumbling, and I let loose this flaming flatulence as I'm cruising down Westcott Street. I know that if I was in a room and had to sit still with that one even I might complain of its rankness. I mean, sometimes when you rip one you like to sit around and bask in its glory because you can be proud that something that usually would only be manufactured by a small, rogue foreign government could come out of your ass. But other times, like right now, usually after Molson or The Beast, or better yet Schlitz, the last thing you want to do is acknowledge that something that foul came from your insides. If that happened without explanation I'd swear it was my body leaking the smell of death.

I make the turn off of Westcott and onto Genesee (I'm taking the scenic route this morning) and this kid driving a brand new Land Rover nearly takes me out. Bastard. I flip him off and he lays on his horn. He's got Jersey plates and a Syracuse University sticker on the back windshield. I want to yell something at him but he's zipping along and is so far out of earshot it's pointless. Besides, he has his windows up: air conditioning.

From Genesee I whip to the right onto Teall, and from there it's a good straight shot downhill with me flanked by stop signs so I don't need to worry about any assholes with a wild hair plowing into me.

In eighth grade a buddy of mine was crossing Erie Boulevard

and got mowed by a Monte Carlo. Broke his leg like you wouldn't believe. Bone was sticking out and everything. I was standing on the other side of the road and I hadn't seen the car coming either. When it hit him he flipped up and onto the windshield. I remember standing there on the sidewalk, looking at him where he had rolled down onto the hood of the car, and I noticed how the windshield hadn't cracked at all like it does in the movies when people get hit by a car. I thought he was dead because he wasn't moving. There was a woman behind the wheel of the car. I could hear her screaming, and then a guy came from out of nowhere. Later I realized he had been in the car behind her. He tapped on her window to get her to roll it down. She was going nuts. Then he checked my friend, and by this time a lot more people had stopped their cars and had gotten out. Traffic was backing up. People who couldn't see were beeping their horns, and then there were sirens. I didn't know what I was supposed to do so I laid my board down and just sat there on it.

But I didn't feel like being there, so I stood up and started kicking it back to my house. A guy a couple of cars down yelled to me: *Hey, what's up?* I told him there had been some accident but I didn't know much more than that, and he waved his hand in thanks, and I went on my way. I didn't go back to my house though. At least not right away. There was an arcade on the way and all day I had been wanting to play Street Fighter. There were some people I went to school with there, and I walked in and was like, *Hey, did you hear? Chris Ward just got the shaft from a Monte Carlo.* I was excited because for once I was the first one with something relevant to tell everyone. Chris ended up okay, though. He was in a body cast for a couple of months, and he had been knocked unconscious so in the end it didn't really matter what I did. I still feel bad about leaving him there. I mean, it was just luck one of his neighbors happened to drive the ambulance, otherwise how would they have known who he was? But it doesn't matter, I guess, since he and I kind of quit hanging out that next year anyway.

I've got the green light at Erie Boulevard today so I ride through the intersection instead of hopping off the board at the median and running through the last two lanes of traffic. Even though it's a bad idea I angle the board towards the A-Plus mart. I think I see Lia behind the counter, and I veer up and away from the store, with the intention of circling the pumps and heading back out onto Teall and down the road to home. But yesterday, before she realized I was the guy with the bowel blowout, I felt there was some spark. She was talking to me like she was interested. She was laughing at my lame jokes. Granted, she crushed me ruthlessly in front of the brooding coffee house crowd, but her brief flirtation is all I've got, and as I'm fond of pointing out, I don't have much.

A guy is at the counter inside and he looks like he's about to exit. If I time it right and I can go skating in the door and I'll look like a real pro. At the end of the pumps, to dress things up for a better gas pumping experience, there are these barrels of flowers. I suppose the barrels are intended to look like planters in an urban mode, but whatever. I kick the board a little faster, grab a flower and put the stem in my mouth. I look up: the person coming out the door kind of steps to the side and holds it for me. This couldn't be more perfect. I'm oriented so I'll be facing Lia as I enter through the doors, and I spread my arms wide and smile with the flower clenched in my mouth as she looks up from the counter at me. This could be the great turning point in my life.

I haven't had much to look forward to for the past several years. As Paul said: it's easy to just get by here. I've been slacking for as long as I can remember. I've had no ambition. I mean, I think I used to, but who knows? And trying to find a poster for your wall is not exactly considered ambitious by the general populace. Maybe that dude that hangs with the Beastie Boys—the Dalai Lama—he might mistake my focus on my search for the perfect poster for my wall as a heightened state of being. Maybe I should get him to talk to my folks.

But that whole thing with Paul the other night, about the guidance counselor, and the dude that offed himself in the McDonald's... That's been in the back of my head, like, what am I doing with my life? I've just been feeling weird lately. Scared maybe that I've got nothing but a ton of comic books, a Battlestar Galactica blanket, and my skate board. Some people I went to high school with are already married and have kids, or they've gone off to college. My mom shows me little clippings in the paper about them getting engaged or winning some scholarship. It's like she's trying to give me a complex in this bizarre passive-aggressive way. Though is there really any better way to give someone a complex? This used to be all well and good. I'd sell a bag of weed every now and again to get some cash, or just borrow it from Paul or Mom and Dad. I don't know why they haven't kicked me out yet. Maybe it's because they were raised in a time when families stuck together. At least that's what mom says—she says families used to stay together for a long time and that it's natural.

And then she'll mention something about how since I'm still living with them, and not working, I should take a couple of classes at the university. But I see how the machine functions: you go off to school, you start getting these ideas that just because you're getting a degree the world is going to be a better place, so you start making plans, you believe you're going to start living the lush life, two cars, house in the suburbs where they keep out the poor people, and then they hand you that piece of paper and it's like you've walked off a cliff, like in that Roadrunner and Coyote cartoon: you've got a split second before you drop back down to earth to realize that your dream life isn't going to happen if you never had it in the first place. If you're like me, by which I mean lower middle class, that's what you're always going to be. At least that's how it is around here. If I go to college I'll just be lower middle class with a chip on my shoulder, because I'll have some sort of certification that entitles me to be an asshole.

Which is why all of this is so important—I'm living in one of the worst cities in the country, I've never been much of anywhere else and probably won't ever, and I don't have a clue what's in the distant future except another bout with my bowels, trying to be more covert about my masturbation, and dying. That's a dismal picture for sure. And just to look into Lia's eyes as I eclipse the door, flower clenched tight in my teeth, arms wide as if to say: *I long only for you, for your tender embrace, the gentle curve of your cheek, and the feel of your skin against mine*—this will make it all bearable.

I'm sprawled out with Twinkies and Ding Dongs all around me. Something about this floor... maybe what it's waxed with... but the second my wheels hit it my board just seemed to fly out from under me, and with the momentum I had I cruised right into a rack of snack cakes. I want to close my eyes right now and just stay here, maybe stop time or something, just anything so I don't have to stand and look like the fool that I am.

"You're trying to make my job more miserable than it already is, aren't you? Is that the aim of your existence now?"

Lia is standing over me, and I raise up on my elbows and say:

"No. Not really."

"Are you retarded? Do you have some sort of learning disability? Are you a visual learner? Should I act out everything I say, maybe draw you a picture?"

I brush some snack cakes off of me, then stand and look at the mess I've made.

"I just wanted, you know, to make an entrance."

"Trying to impress me?"

I feel my face go red. "Maybe I should pick these up."

"Because if you're trying to impress me, you have. You've impressed upon me the fact that you are deranged. Do you know there's such a thing as anti-stalking laws? I could take you to court. This might have been considered romantic in the days of leeches and iron maidens and the plague, but such violations of a woman's space are generally viewed as criminal now."

I open my mouth to say something but once again she has rendered me speechless. I hang my head and start gathering Twinkies in my arms and putting them back on the little wire racks that I crashed into. Maybe tonight Megan and I can go to Phoebe's Garden Cafe and have a nice dinner. Her dad usually lets her borrow the car for these kind of things. I think I need to double down on what I've already got. Paul can front me a few more bucks. Then Megan and I can rent a movie and go back to her folks' place and see what happens. Maybe I haven't been patient enough. Maybe tonight we can get it right.

"Hey."

I turn around and Lia is watching me.

"Yeah?"

"Not a big fan of SkaCago?"

"What?"

"You left at the set break last night."

"Oh, right. Yeah, that band sucked."

She reaches in her front pants pocket and takes out a pack of Kools and lights one up. Forget about Megan. This is definitely something. I've got the mojo working. She has fallen for the charms of a man going headlong into a rack of snack cakes, despite what she may have said.

"I had a cousin that was slow like you. You seem to get by okay though. You've got friends, right?"

I don't say anything.

"You can find your way home and stuff, right?"

"Yeah."

"Good boy." Even though she's making fun of me there is

something about the way she says it, like she is genuinely pleased with me; it makes my insides hum. "So I guess you can find your way around? You must be able to, otherwise you wouldn't be out. Do you know where 425 Ackerman is?"

"I can figure it out."

"Do I need to write it down for you?"

I frown. She smiles, takes a puff from her cigarette.

"Party tonight," she says. "Show up around ten or so. You can tell time?"

I frown at her again.

"There's a keg. Bring your friends in case you get lost or need some help going to the bathroom. I'm not going to give you any help there. I've seen the damage you can do."

I feel as though I should respond to the bathroom comment, but I heard on some talk show that sometimes the most tactful way to handle a rude comment is to ignore it. Unfortunately, this strategy seems only to work in places where they serve little triangle shaped pimento cheese sandwiches with the crust trimmed off. I say:

"Just make sure to leave an extra roll of paper on the back of the tank and we won't have any problems."

She smiles and takes the last drag of her cigarette, then puts it out. Lia says:

"You can go now. I have to stock the gum."

I grab my board and start for the door. This isn't exactly shaping up according to my master plan, but maybe this lovable goofball schtick is the angle I should have been taking my whole life. It seems to be producing results. I wonder why I didn't think of this before.

"Hey!"

I turn around, raise my eyebrows.

"It's store policy to ask the name of every person who disrespects our lavatory facilities, just in case they become repeat offenders. I forgot the other day. You understand. I was a little caught off guard by your utter stupidity and complete lack of respect in trying to skip out. So let's have it."

"Jordan. Jordan Flint."

"Well, Jordan Flint, make sure you bring along your girlfriend."

Dad's already in bed when I get home. I can hear my sister's stereo down the hall playing the Violent Femmes. You know, that one album everyone has. It should be a medical condition that everyone between the ages of sixteen and eighteen buys *that one album* to hear *that one song*. That said, that album is a masterpiece.

I drink some juice straight out of the carton, which I know is completely an uncool thing to do since other people live here, but it's my own family, right? If I had something contagious they'd probably end up with it anyway. And like my sister hasn't gone out and blown a guy and then come in and drank straight from the carton without performing a little Listerine ritual. I close up the carton and put it back in the fridge and take an Eggo waffle out of the freezer and drop it in the toaster.

I turn on the portable TV and Springer is on. I love this show. There are few things more satisfying in life than watching big haired women all hopped up on Salon Selective tearing each other to pieces because they just found out that they've been sharing the same greaseball boyfriend for months. Seeing this stuff makes me glad I come from a relatively normal family: my parents are frigid, my sister is a slut, and I'm completely smitten with one girl, yet dating another. No doubt it's everything my immigrant ancestors dreamt was possible.

But I can't watch Springer right now. I flip the channel through Sally Jesse and Regis and Judge Judy, but it's no good. I'm going out of my mind here: I just want to know what it all means.

The whole way here from the A-Plus Mart I've been trying to sort out the implications of what happened between me and Lia. I mean, she invites me to this party, and I'd swear that when I was picking up those Twinkies there was some full-on flirting going on. But she knows I have a chick, and not only does she know, she reminds me to bring her to this shindig tonight. You see? This is why the world is so screwed up. No one can just come out with it. It has to be this game, this freaking game that just puts my bowels into knots. I don't even want my Eggo anymore. I leave it in the toaster and head back to my room. I'll call Paul later and let him know we've got things to do tonight. He'll come. He always does, without question. That's one of the things I love about the guy. And maybe we can sort out the mystery that is Lia before we get there so I can have a strategy.

I flop on my bed, suddenly very tired, but it's one of those so-tired-you-can't-sleep scenarios. I get up and put a Rollins Band tape in my stereo. Whenever girls have me down I like the sanity of Rollins to ground me. I lie back down on my bed and I cup my nuts in my left hand, trying to think of all the scenarios that could go down tonight. Rollins belts out: *You didn't need to do that to me.* Yeah. I start getting a half shaft and the urge to beat it, so I take my hand off of my nads and curl both my arms under my pillow and try not to think about anything at all.

"Jordan."

My dad has his hand on my shoulder, shaking me. The sun is still blazing outside my window so it has to be early afternoon. Usually dad is still asleep at this hour so this can't be good. I try to make myself look as innocent as possible, just in case, and I say, "Yeah?" He says:

"I think you need to come in the kitchen. We need to talk."

He turns and goes out of my room, down the hall, and I wearily pull myself out of bed and follow. I really don't want to be up; everything has that wigged-out vibe, like you're stoned or drunk or not even a part of the world and your body is just going on autopilot. I don't like dealing with people when I'm feeling like this because there's no telling what I might say or do.

Dad is standing in the middle of the kitchen, his arms crossed, staring at the floor. Kelly is sitting at the table. She looks up at me, then back down to her hands folded in her lap. Dad inhales deeply and then he says:

"You know, I work hard. Real hard to keep a roof over your mother's head and mine, and I let you all live here because you're my children, and because it would break your mother's heart if I kicked you both out. And don't think I haven't thought about it. The two of you are at each other all the time, and it causes your mom and me a good deal of grief. Her more than me, because you all could tear each other to pieces and I wouldn't care because you're both adults. The point where I start to care is when the problems that the two of you have with one another start to interfere with my life. I'm getting old. I'm done with you. If you like living here for free and eating my food—because it is all mine—you're going to have to start doing it by my rules." He turns to me, looks me square in the eye like I just buggered his dog and shot it. "Jordan, for you that means you're going to get a job and stop sleeping all day. You need to grow up and start demonstrating that you can be responsible. I look at how you've turned out and it disappoints me. This degenerate behavior of yours ends right now. You're sister woke me up crying, and apparently you are the cause. She told me something that I find very disturbing, and I'd like an explanation."

I look over at Kelly but she's not looking at me. I can't believe this. If I knew my bathroom incident was going to lead to a family crisis I would have saved it and just let Megan take care of me later that night. Besides that, I can't believe what my dad is saying: I'm not allowed to masturbate in his house? Or maybe he means just the bathroom since we all share it. That I could understand, but what a strange conversation to be having anyway. I'm kind of glad I'm still half asleep because if I was totally awake I would turn around and go back to my room, shut the door, and slit my wrists. Dad says:

"Well? What is it? Do you think you can go around behaving anyway you please in this house?"

"Look," I say, "I'm sorry. I won't let it happen again."

Dad puts his hands on his hips and looks at the floor and shakes his head. He doesn't look at me when he speaks:

"I'd like to believe you, Jordan, but I just can't. You've been doing this and stuff like it for years. I tell your mother it's just a phase that all boys your age go through. I went through it. Your grandfather went through it. We laugh about it now, sure. Hell, I think even your mother, when I first met her, was a little less uptight than she is now. And that's why I haven't said anything until now. You're going to be twenty-one soon. You'll be a full-fledged adult and you're going to have to start acting like one. This needs to stop."

I'm blown away by all this. I know after I've gone back to sleep and woken up again I'm going to wonder if this was all a dream. Your dad isn't supposed to discuss masturbation with you, especially not in front of your sister. I say:

"Dad, I'm sorry, I'm really, really sorry. It won't happen again." I feel like I'm about to cry out of embarrassment.

He gives me that look again, like I'm trying to sell him on the idea that the world is flat.

"Okay. Against my better judgment I'm going to take you at your word. I figure being my boy you've got some will power in you. You can put a stop to this behavior right now. But Jordan, mind you, if this ever happens again—" he plucks the Eggo Waffle from the toaster "—I'm going to have to ask you to leave, no matter how much it hurts your mother. Now apologize to your sister. She spent a lot of time cleaning this kitchen, and there you go doing something like this and demonstrating a complete lack of respect for her."

Jesus.

Dad comes in my room while I'm trying to go back to sleep. I have my back to the door, but I know it's him by the slow gait he has and the way the floor creaks with his weight. He shuts the door behind him and says quietly:

"You awake?"

I consider not answering because things have already been too bizarre for my tastes today. It's not as bizarre as the other day by a long shot, but still... Sometimes I feel like my life is just one huge auto-accident: you really can't take any pleasure in it, but it's hard not to look at the carnage and feel somewhat giddy. I say:

"Yeah."

"I know I came off like a hard-ass out there, and you know how I feel about you getting a job. And you need to pick up after yourself around here. Your mom and your sister aren't your servants. But I came down on you like that because your sister seemed a damned wreck over that waffle. I just want to get to bed myself and not have to listen to any more of her bawling, you know?"

The whole time he's talking he's very matter of fact, as though he were speaking about the weather.

"Look," he says, "I think your sister is on her period, or just about to be, because when I came back from the gym last night she was acting all weird, and she was up again this morning when I came home from work. And now there's this thing with the waffle. And I don't think it's really all about a waffle, do you?"

He doesn't wait for an answer.

"No, something is up. Maybe this whole business with the McDonald's has her scared. It makes sense. She's a young woman, vulnerable. Things like this can make a person wonder about how safe the world is. Your mother used to worry about these things when we first got married." He stops. For a second I think he's wandered out of the room, but I hear him take a breath.

"When we first were married some towel heads hijacked a plane. Your mother had never been on a plane. I'd never been on a plane, and I didn't see any cause for us to start, but she was worried sick about what might happen if we ever did. It was the sweetest thing you ever saw. Of course at the time it drove me up one wall and down the other. But now..." I'm waiting for him to finish. I hear him fiddling with the door knob. "Did you know this was loose?"

"No."

"I'll have to get a screw driver to tighten that. Anyway, I know you and Kelly don't get along for one reason or another, but why don't you see if you can put that behind you for a little while and see what's up. If it has something to do with this McDonald's business, or this guy she's seeing and staying with some nights, well, that's one thing. But if it's something serious, like marijuana, or cough syrup, I want to know."

Oh, the conclusion of every parent of children in the last 20 years! If your kid is a malcontent it *must be* because they're high. Don't they know? It's the drugs that keep us sane. You'll never see anyone who's stoned picking up a rifle and whacking a busload of kids on their way to interfaith camp. Well, with the exception of our neighborhood shooter the other day. But I don't think that counts. He was tampering with the commercial stuff, and who knows what they put in those demon cocktails? Having experienced it myself I'm beginning to wonder. I turn to dad:

"Kelly's seeing someone?"

"I thought you knew."

He starts back toward the door and I say:

"I doubt she's on drugs."

"Why do you say that?"

"I don't know."

"Well." He says it like we've settled something. I lay my head down as he goes out the door, and I feel like trying to sort all of this out, but I've got enough on my mind already.

CHAPTER EIGHT

We Are Rolling

I HEAR PAUL'S VOICE LIKE I'm standing in a large airplane hanger, like he's fifty feet away from me.

"You sure this is the place?"

But now it seems like Paul said those words an hour ago. My body feels like it's humming, and it's not as humid outside as it has been. Or maybe it is. I can't tell, but it feels good, regardless. And then I hear myself saying:

"I don't know. What did I say? 425? Maybe it's 524. Did I say 425?"

I'm just standing and looking at the house, and Craig and Megan are laughing behind me. I turn slowly, like I'm twisting in water. They're laughing and Megan is holding onto his arm like she's about to fall over. Paul says to Lourdene:

"What did he say?"

I'm waiting for her to answer. This is hopeless. I feel rational, but only in my head, like things won't make sense outside of me no matter how hard I try. Lourdene says:

"Let's go in."

"But what if this isn't the place?" Paul doesn't look worried, though, when he says it, and the way he says it is like: *So what if it isn't? We'll just turn around and go out and no harm done.*

"Hear it?"

I can't hear anything besides Craig and Megan laughing, or somebody yelling down the street. I think I hear somebody yelling down the street but I'm not sure, because no one else seems to be hearing it. Paul says:

"Yeah, I guess this is it."

They start towards the house and I follow, but Craig and Megan aren't moving, so I say:

"Hey," and they start to move without even looking at me, like everything I needed to convey I boiled down to one syllable. Unbelievable. My eyelids are fluttering.

We're almost at the front door of the house when the sounds of screaming down the street stop and I realize that what I'm hearing is music coming from inside. I want to say it's The Cure, which in most circumstances would have me looking for an exit, but right now I love all music. My head commands me to love all music. Music is good. The Cure is music, therefore The Cure must be good.

I follow Paul and Lourdene into the house which is dimly lit with lamps draped with tapestries. Everything seems to be covered in some sort of paisley cloth. Above the lamps you can make out the heavy hang of smoke and I smell reefer burning. I can't tell if anyone is looking at us, and instead of stopping inside the door to check things out we press on, like we always do, afraid to look too conspicuous. Paul and Lourdene cut a path through the living room and a guy I pass looks at me while smoking his cigarette and raises his head like he knows me. I smile and say, "What's up, man." I look down at his t-shirt. It's red, with the familiar Golden Arches drawn in yellow marker, and written underneath is a single word: *McPsycho*.

We walk down a hallway and pass a few people in one room who are sitting on a bed; one of them has a bong pressed to his mouth. We end up in the kitchen which is bright with florescent lights. There's a keg over in the corner. Paul hands me and Lourdene a plastic cup and starts pumping the keg.

"Dude." I hold out my cup and he draws me a foamy beer.

"Where's Craig and Megan?"

I look behind me, even though I'm standing against a wall, and in my head I can hear myself saying, *You knew you were up against a wall,* but it seems like I didn't, or I don't remember getting there, and I look at Paul, shrug my shoulders. Lourdene says:

"Someone rub my head." Paul looks at me. I say:

"I don't know." I think I can still hear them laughing, but I shake my head and it goes away. The tips of my fingers feel tingly. Paul starts rubbing Lourdene's head. I want someone to rub my head now, too.

A woman who looks a little bit older than me is leaning against the kitchen counter, holding a beer and kind of bobbing her head to the music. She has a strip of pink cascading down through her brown hair, and I think how happy that is. I mean, that's just the happiest thing I've ever seen, this bit of pink in her hair. It tickles me, right inside my stomach, which, as I understand, has a pink hue to it. I mean, I'm just tickled pink. Paul says:

"Kiss me."

"What?"

"Not you."

"Oh." Lourdene kisses him. I think my heart might normally sink right about now at the ease of their intimacy, but I feel only joy for them. I love drugs. Paul steps back from Lourdene and gives me a hug, then pulls back and rubs my shoulders. Bliss.

"So, big fat cat, where's it at, baby?"

"I don't know." I've got it in my head now: *Big fat cat where's it at? Big fat cat where's it at? Big fat cat where's it at?* I say:

"I think I'm going to puke, dude."

The woman with the pink stripe in her hair says:

"The bathroom is down the hall and on your left."

I take a step. I am fine. False alarm.

We walk out into the hall and back the way we came, into the living room and towards the front door, weaving our way around people I can just barely make sense of. I feel so far set back in my head, like this isn't me walking and I am disconnected from the world. I'm walking up steps and I only realize it when I trip on one and spill some of my beer on a girl's shoe and she says:

"Hey," but I don't stop to apologize because if I do I don't think I'll get moving again.

I bump into Paul at the top of the stairs. He and Lourdene have stopped moving and I can feel my body rooting where it is so I say:

But nothing comes out. I can't open my jaw. I'm clenching my teeth and I don't want to stop clenching them because it feels so good. This stuff we took tonight, Blue Love, is kicking my ass. I don't normally take ecstasy, but Lourdene got this from her brother and bought enough for everyone, even Brenda and Lara who didn't show up because they're out with some guys they met the other night at the Tri-Delt house. Craig and Megan took the extra two which is probably why I can't find them—they've zoned out somewhere.

And on top of this we smoked. Paul has a pipe with a bowl made of ivory and it's carved to look like an Indian Guru sitting with his legs crossed. It's the tits as far as pipes go. It even has a name: Rosebud. Every time we smoke from that pipe Paul makes a point to say: *So look, when I die, and my last word is Rosebud, you guys don't have to go around scratching your heads—I'm talking about my bowl.* He packed a big fat bud in the bowl and told me that it was all mine. Which usually I'm down with, but after the first toke I knew it was going to destroy me on top of the ecstasy, but what can you do? I couldn't back down because I'd never hear the end of it. But now I'm wishing I had said, *Look, I've got to keep my head tonight around this girl.* But like the idiot I usually am I've set myself up for probable failure. I'm going to look like a tool whenever I find Lia. A happy tool, but a tool nonetheless.

I lean forward against Paul's back and start twisting my head around and it feels so good. Someone grabs my arm. That feels good too.

"Bring any for me?"

I turn around and Lia is standing there. I just look at her.

"I guess not."

My whole body feels like it has come alive, and there is music inside me, vibrating and singing. She takes my hand and leads me down the steps. I want to say, *Megan might*—or something like that, but I don't know how to finish it, or I do know, but it's too slow getting through my head and when it comes time to let the words ease from my lips it doesn't seem worth the effort, so I just let myself be dragged back down the stairs, through the living room and back into the kitchen. I look for Megan the whole way but I don't see her, though I might have just missed her with it being so dark and the way the music seems to hide everything. I don't know where my beer went. The pink stripe woman is still there, nodding to the music. She looks up and smiles. Lia says:

"Jordan, this is Carol."

I muster up a *Hi*, and then I start to giggle because I really am. Carol says to Lia:

"We've already met. He was going to puke."

"It figures." She frowns at me and shakes her head. "We're going up on the roof."

"Be careful. And don't let anyone else up there."

"Don't worry, mom." Lia takes my hand again and leads me out a door to another set of stairs at the back of the house that are strewn with cobwebs. Or are they? My vision is fluttery, compromised. I just now realize what was said, so I say:

"Was that really your mom?"

Lia doesn't say anything, just turns to me and shakes her

head again. I'm beginning to fall in love with that head shaking. A few seconds later she says:

"Watch your head."

But I bang it anyway going into a dark room which I guess is the attic. Lia flips on a single bare bulb which gives the place the glow of a sparse cell in Central America where infidels and communists are executed. I feel more detached from myself than I did before. We walk to the end of the room and she opens a window and steps out and disappears. I don't move. Her head pops back in the window and she says:

"Well?"

I step out onto the roof. It's a lot higher than I thought it would be, and I follow her around and over to the chimney. There's a place there where the roof line comes together at a ninety-degree angle, and she lays down on her back. I do the same. The shingles, with their rough surface, feel divine against my back, like hundreds of fingers gently scratching me, and the roof is still slightly warm from the afternoon sun. We're lying where the streetlights don't bleed in so we're shrouded in near darkness.

I don't know how long we've been here. It feels like a long time because I hear the music change inside. There's a woman singing and a lot of nasty guitar. My eyes close. I'm not picturing anything, just feeling good. So good. Being out of myself. Somewhere a bottle smashes. Lia says:

"I saw you brought your girlfriend. She was with some other guy."

"Craig. Good guy."

"She's very pretty."

"She's a good girl." I wish I hadn't gotten so wasted. I don't feel like I can make sense beyond myself. I want to be smooth. I want to say something along the lines of, *Yeah, she's hot. But not as hot as you,* but that seems stupid. Or does it? I can't be sure. This girl isn't stupid. I open my eyes. Lia's face is right above mine, maybe three inches away. She's looking into my eyes. She says:

"I have to pee."

"Okay."

"Wait here."

She scoots down the roof line until she's almost at the edge. She has her back to me. At the edge of the roof she pulls up the dress she's wearing—I hadn't really noticed it until now. It's a long flowing dress like hippie girls wear. I hear her pee hit the shingles on the roof and run into the gutter. I don't guess she's wearing underwear. I close my eyes and I can feel myself getting an erection. Not that I'm some kinky freak who gets off on watching girls pee or anything like that, but I just know she's got her dress pulled up and she's not wearing any panties and it's a complete turn on you understand. I imagine her crawling back up the roof to me, undoing my shorts, pulling off her dress, and us doing it right here on the roof with everyone below us getting wasted and being none the wiser.

I feel her hair on my face. I open my eyes and she's leaning over me again:

"What are you afraid of?"

Normally I'd say I was afraid of heights, but I don't say that right now because I'm feeling so good, and heights are good, and I really don't know this girl. She could respond to my fear of heights by rolling me off this roof right now for tormenting her the past few days. But it wasn't torment. It was a display of affection. Affection is good, and people who respond to it are good, and this girl is good. But I still keep the heights thing to myself. I say:

"I don't know. Dying, I guess." I immediately realize this isn't a significantly better answer.

She lays down beside me and I stare up at the sky. I can make out what might be stars against the black, or it might be air planes or satellites. I'm not really sure. The only time I've seen the sky full of stars was when my family used to go out to my grandmother's place. I remember one night we built a bonfire on the beach and cooked hot-dogs on a stick and, later on, marshmallows. I took one hot, gooey marshmallow and chunked it at my sister and burned her arm with it; I don't think mom or dad did anything. At least not anything I remember, even though Kelly cried a lot. I know this is sounding like the Brady Bunch Summer Vacation Special, like we were sitting around belting out "Our House" and just absolutely boohooed when we had to tell each other goodnight and how much we loved one another. Trust me: it wasn't like that at all.

Mom and dad laid on a blanket and made out, which is kind of creepy now that I think about it, doing that in front of Kelly and me. Being so young I doubt either of us would have known if they were humping each other silly. But anyway, while they were doing that, and after Kelly forgot that I had nearly branded her with a scalding hot marshmallow, she and I kind of splashed around in the cold water. After that we threw sticks or rocks or whatever we could find back in the lake.

When the fire had died down and mom and dad were asleep (or pretending to sleep), Kelly and I sat on a rock that jutted out into the water. Dad told us earlier not to go out on it because we might fall in, hit our heads and drown and not be found in the dark. So how could we resist after that kind of scare tactic? We lay back and for the first time I really paid attention to the fact that there were all these stars in the sky that I had never seen before. I mean, the water just seemed to be shimmering with them. Kelly curled against me and we stayed there for a while looking up at the night sky and listening to the water splash up against the rock. Until dad figured out where we were and started screaming like razors were dripping out of his ass. That was one of those spankings I remember. Kelly didn't take any heat that night because I was the oldest, thus it was my responsibility to listen to dad's instructions and obey his commands. I recall she fell down laughing while dad chased me around with his belt. So much for the bonding moment we had.

"Ski-lifts in summer."

I hear this voice inside my head talking about ski-lifts in summer. It's the weirdest thing, because I can see the beach in front of my grandmother's house at the lake, and there are these ski-lifts just stretching down the shore and the people carrier things are empty and just swinging back and forth.

CHAPTER NINE

Inertia

I DON'T CARE IF IT'S your intention to fall asleep on a roof—it is the most disorienting experience when you wake up on one.

At first I thought I was dreaming, but everything had become suddenly vivid: I was very aware of my body and of being in it. Most often when I dream I feel as if I'm watching myself in a movie. Sometimes I get that way when I'm awake, too: I seem to stumble through the day feeling like I'm not even a part of myself. It's this town. Nothing ever changes and your life becomes a rut to the point where you don't even have to participate.

I'm pressed flat against the shingles on my stomach, which doesn't feel as good as it did earlier. I don't recall being on my stomach when I was out here with Lia, so I must have rolled over in my sleep, which is really freaking me out because what if I'd rolled right off the roof? I am not what you might call a sound sleeper. I tend to thrash about for some reason, and about once a week I roll off whatever bed or couch I'm sleeping on.

I raise my head and look around the roof—I don't see Lia anywhere. This is no good. I had a feeling that this girl might be nuts, but the ecstasy washed it right out of my head. This could have been disastrous; it might be yet. I'm just glad I woke up. I hate drugs.

I start inching my way slowly to my left. I'm not sure why I'm going left, but this seems like the way to go—call it instinct. Waking up like this has made me extremely aware of everything. I mean, I can smell the soft rot working away beneath these shingles. I can smell the stale beer stench of the party. Someone is shuffling down the street. A tree limb is creaking. All the hairs on my body feel as though they have lifted in unison. This is twisted. I remember reading somewhere that florescent lights aren't on in one continual wave of light, that they flicker faster than our eyes can detect. But I'd swear right now I can make out the subtle breaks in the waves of light coming off of the street lamps. I'm looking at my hand against the dark gray of the shingles, and for the first time I'm really noticing that this is my hand. It's coming from me, and I'm watching all those tiny things you never notice happening with it—tendons and muscles on the back of it, these small movements. I've got a cut across two of my knuckles and I'm not even sure how I got it. It almost looks like a huge canyon slicing across the landscape of my hand. But it's just a scratch really, and yet it's this tear in this whole other world which is my body.

It's possible I'm still fairly lit.

I've got to get off this fucking roof.

I start moving to my left again, hugging close to the roof and feeling the grit from the shingles scrape my arms and legs as I do so. I'm beginning to think that maybe left isn't the way to go. And I can't call for help. People call for help all the time around here and no one pays any attention because they figure it's just some crackhead or college prick all hopped up. Besides, if someone did actually listen for once they'd call the cops and everyone still crashed out inside would get busted for weed or underage drinking or something along those lines, and Lia would be pissed and then I'd be *that guy*. This is a serious dilemma.

"You all right?"

I look to my right but no one is there. I am definitely still wasted. I'm having auditory hallucinations. If the voice tells me to jump I will not abide.

"Behind you."

"I don't believe you. There's nothing behind me but a drop off and I'm not jumping so get out of my head."

The voice doesn't say anything else. Which is fine by me, and personally I'm feeling pretty good about being able to master my hallucinations. They say that being able to do that is the sign of a solid psyche.

"What?"

Crap.

"Look, I'm not going to jump."

"I don't know what you're talking about."

It's funny, though, because when I've imagined what the voice inside my head might sound like, I've always imagined my own voice. Or anything but this voice, which sounds like a well-educated Foghorn Leghorn.

"Look, would you at least just roll over. I don't like talking to the back of your head."

Against my better judgment I roll over; I'm curious to see where this all is leading.

"That's better. I know what you're thinking, but let me assure you: I'm no morning person either. But how could I resist her: the morning star in all her glory."

An old man is perched on the roof opposite me. He's got a platform set up so there's a flat place where he has a telescope aimed skyward. Which is cool, I guess, but personally I've always wanted a telescope so I could aim it in my neighbors' windows to see if anything worth my time was going on. The old guy says:

"I would have said something earlier but you seemed to be sleeping."

"Yeah. I was. I guess."

"Were you waiting on Venus?"

"What?"

"I guess not. The planet. Venus. She's at her best right now."

"I never much went for that stuff."

He shrugs his shoulders and puts his eye to the small end of the telescope and screws around with something on the side of it. He asks:

"They teach you astronomy in school?"

I don't answer him. I raise up and start looking around, wondering how I got up here in the first place. It seemed pretty easy just stepping out onto the roof. But who can say? I was pretty toasted.

"In school, son. They teach you astronomy? You know: stars and planets?"

I get the distinct feeling that this old dude is talking down to me. I feel like saying: *Hey, Grandpa Munster, blow me.*

But I don't like giving old people a hard time. They're on their way out and they must know it. I don't suppose that's an easy thing to face. I know I'm going to die and there's nothing I can do about it, but I don't like the idea of it all. I don't like the idea of giving up *me*. I don't really believe in heaven or hell. I think this is it, and you have to make your play here or not at all. I've got time. But old people, well, it's over. You either made it or you didn't, and if you didn't I suspect that's a major downer to come to terms with. Especially if you have to wear one of those adult diapers. Is there anything more humiliating than failing at life *and* wetting yourself all the time? I think not.

I say:

"I'm not in school."

He doesn't respond, just looks through the telescope. Then:

"I guess you caught Hale-Bop?"

"No. Where did they play?"

He jerks his head away from the eye piece and I have the notion that he's squinting at me.

"You doped up, boy? Is that why you're on the roof? Because you were smoking dope with the reefers and got so out of your mind you ended up on the roof?"

"What are you talking about?"

"Hale-Bopp, the comet. What else? See, that dope you're doing is already fogging your brain, son. You've got to keep your head clear so you can make your way in the world."

I don't know what to say. What's the point? It's... I don't know, bum fuck in the morning, some old guy's on his roof—*I'm on a roof.* It's past the point of being able to say anything.

But he's not saying anything either and it's making me uncomfortable with the silence between us. Like I always do in situations such as these I break down.

"What comet?"

He shakes his head at me. He clears his throat and I hear him hock up the most massive lugie. And then he just lets it loose. I hear that perfect sound of spit and phlegm bonded together and leaving a rounded mouth: and then nothing. I wish it were brighter so I could see the arc on that thing and watch its final descent before it smacks the pavement. Which it does: it's magnificent, sitting up here on the roof and hearing it crack against the concrete, like a tiny god clapping his hands together. I want to cry out: *Solid Gold you old coot! What a whopper!* But I feel that would be inappropriate at this point in our relationship so I stay quiet. The old man says:

"Hale-Bop came through a couple of months ago. Pretty bright in the sky, even with all the lights around here. Bunch of people out in California cut their nuts off and killed themselves because of it."

"If I cut my nuts off I'd whack myself, too."

The old guy laughs a little under his breath, but he's shaking his head again too, so I'm not quite sure where I stand on this one.

"They didn't kill themselves because they cut their nuts off. They cut their nuts off and killed themselves because they thought the comet was a spaceship coming to take them to the next world."

"Well, that's pretty sinister."

Come to think of it, though, I do have the vague recollection that I've heard about all this. I seem to remember my dad going off about a bunch of weirdos that cut their nads off because of aliens, or something to that effect. He was on a supreme rant about it: this was the perfect example of the problem with teaching sex-ed in school and gays being out in the open. (*Not, of course,* he was quick to add, *that there's anything wrong with that, but I was raised to keep your business private*). As soon as you give kids condoms and teach them about homosexuality they go crazy because it's not natural and they end up castrating themselves. That was his take on it. My dad has some interesting ideas. I'm thankful that he elects not to share most of them but opts instead to mutter them under his breath as he walks out of a room.

"Well, I suppose a lot of people have funny ideas about how to get to the next world, or about how they're going to be saved. Can't hold them all accountable."

"They should have held onto their balls and put them to good use in the world that counts."

The old guy fiddles with his telescope again, not saying anything. I need to get off this roof, so I say:

But he gets in ahead of me:

"What makes you think this is the only world that counts?"

Okay. Here we go:

"Look, I don't need a sermon. I was dragged to church by my teeth as a kid by my mom and dad, and finally they came to their senses and just quit going. And let me tell you: I've heard it all, and until I have definitive proof otherwise I am resolved that this is all there is."

"I'm not trying to convert you. I don't care what you believe. I'm a card carrying Deist myself."

"Oh. Okay. Cool." I don't have the slightest clue what he's talking about.

"See all this?" He waves his hand around toward the sky. "God did all this. It's beautiful. There's nothing more beautiful than a clear, starry night. It fills one with the sense of something greater than ourselves. The problem is—" and he makes this big sweeping gesture at all the houses "—the problem is us. We're why you can't make out all the stars in the Big Dipper. You know the ancient Greeks counted two hundred and seven stars in that constellation with the naked eye? How many can we see? Seven. Seven lousy stars because of all the Goddamned lights from the houses and street lights and buildings... Do I think if I prayed every day to God for the rest of my life that he would smite them? No. God doesn't give a rat's ass about any of what we do. Why would he? Of what great concern are we? You'd never catch me cutting my testicles off, that's for sure. But son, I'd sooner believe there was a spaceship behind some comet than the Holy Ghost himself."

This guy is off his rocker.

"Jefferson was a Deist. So were Franklin and Washington. Amazing men. You hear all of this crap about our founding Christian Fathers... Bull. Those were men that knew that God was too busy to mess with us. He just set things in motion and left us all to the basic physics of the universe."

For a second I really wasn't too sure of who this guy was talking about, but I've caught onto it now. And maybe he's not so off his rocker after all. I mean, Jefferson and Franklin, those guys smoked a lot of dope. They knew it was the way to go even back then. Washington I'm not sure about. The guy *was* military.

"They teach you physics in school?"

"I'm not in school anymore."

"I'm telling you, son, you need to stay in school. Plan on spending the rest of your days here?"

"So."

"Goddamn. I didn't see it until now, but now I see it. You know what you are?"

This should be priceless. The old man points two crooked fingers at me:

"You are a victim of inertia."

I'm waiting for a little more here but I don't think it's coming. The guy has gone back to his telescope, making little noises to himself. I've had about enough of him. I don't think I was ever lectured to this much in one day when I was in school, and I'm not at all in the mood to sit through a tutorial on physics. Besides, I never much went for all that stuff. I never went for much of anything now that I think about it.

In tenth grade I had a biology teacher who looked like a famished mouse and had the temperament of a bulldog with inflamed hemorrhoids. She put me off of science. We had to dissect these fetal pigs as our final exam. I mean, the whole term the class had been gathering this momentum towards dissecting the pigs, these little things that looked like a deflated football with eyes and a tail. I made it through the cricket and the frog just fine. Mainly because you can't really relate to crickets and frogs too much; they aren't mammals. But there I was, perched over my fetal pig with a scalpel and my lab partner Elizabeth nearly drooling for me to make the first incision.

I don't know what it was but I couldn't do it. I started thinking about being younger and how I used to read that book *Charlotte's Web* to my sister. This was before she could read, and it took us about a week to get through the whole book, reading a little every night before she went to sleep. Sometimes I would read it to her out in the living room in front of the fire place, and mom and dad would come in and listen to me, correcting me when I would get a word wrong. So there I was looking at that pig, and I knew it was already dead, but this was about the time that mom found the lump in her breast and the doctor told her it was cancer. I didn't know what was going to happen to her. All I knew was that she would be going in for surgery soon, and someone would be taking a scalpel like the one I held in my hand at that moment and would be slicing into her skin. And I just couldn't cut that little pig because of Wilbur who was an orphan and the memory of me sitting there with my sister reading *Charlotte's Web*, and how we might be orphaned soon as well if the surgeon didn't get all the cancer. So I just let loose right there in biology, crying my eyes out.

In retrospect it's one of the things I regret most in my life. I wish I would've had the good sense to have left the room, but when a fit of hysteria hits you like that what are you supposed to do? I never even cried when I was sliding down a twenty foot rail and my board went out from under me and I racked my nuts for ten feet. Needless to say, people don't take that into account when you weep uncontrollably like a little girl with a skinned knee at the sight of a formaldehyde moistened dead little piggy.

But I stood there, rooted in place, making some half-assed attempt to hide the fact that I was losing it. Everyone was quiet. Then they started to giggle, and Mrs. Kirby, like an absolute Nazi, was in my ear telling me to cut that pig like a man. I just shook my head no, over and over, and finally, under her breath, I swear to you she called me a pussy. Can you believe that? I mean, in a way, I don't blame her. Looking back on the whole thing I wish I could teleport through time to that classroom that afternoon, march right up to my younger self and smack the crap out of him. But of course that's not possible according to *Time Cop*: the same matter cannot occupy the same space.

Anyway, the fact is my science teacher called me a pussy, and I was lead to the principle's office where a sorry, red faced old man just looked at me and sighed. And not because, I think, he gave a rat's ass, but really because he didn't. Everyone knew this guy was two years from retirement and would be spending the rest of his life raising cabbage somewhere further upstate. The last thing he wanted to deal with was some sniffling punk. Mrs. Kirby was demanding that I be punished. For what? I don't know. But I was. I was suspended for three days. Actually, I took a week because mom and dad were worked up over her cancer and didn't have a clue as to what I was doing. Still, I managed a D+ in biology, but that was the last time I ever did well in a science class.

"Yeah, I doubt you're going much of anywhere now that I think about it."

"What?" I'd forgotten that the old dude was there.

"I said I guess you're stuck here."

"I'll get down off this roof one way or another."

"Look what that dope has done to your head, son. You can't hold a thought for thirty seconds. What I mean is, I doubt you're going to get over this inertia you've got."

I've had it. I start edging my way back towards where I woke up to see if maybe there's another way down on the other side.

"Don't they teach you anything in school? Newton's First Law? An object at rest tends to stay at rest, or, if moving, tends to stay moving in the same direction unless affected by some outside force. That's what I've been trying to get across to you all along. We've all been left to basic physics, and all these people praying at their kitchen tables at night are waiting for something that isn't there to get them moving. And you, my boy, are about as big a victim of inertia as I've ever seen. If you're lucky, I imagine at best you might just end up like that fellow that shot up the McDonald's the other day. Now there was a man with a vision and the momentum to carry it out. I doubt you've got it in you to do even that."

I crawl up the apex of the house—it looks like there's a window that you can get into if you crawl down a little bit and step on a ledge. I slide over the peak and start scooting down to the ledge. The old man is fiddling with his telescope again. I consider leaving him with a final thought, mainly to kiss my ass. But what's the use?

I have a vague recollection now of coming out of this window earlier, but I don't remember it being as complicated a process as it is now trying to get back in. The ledge in front of the window feels like it slants at a steeper angle than the rest of the roof, so I'm afraid I'm going to take a tumble. I mean, I'm still feeling a little wonky from the ecstasy and the weed. My equilibrium is not operating at peak performance.

I flip myself onto my stomach and slide down onto the ledge to where the tips of my toes are just touching it. Don't get the idea that I'm some kind of ninja. The upper half of my body is still on the roof, so it's only a short drop. I take a hand and grab the edge of the window, then slide the rest of the way down. I feel like I'm being pulled backwards and my one arm that's holding the window gets twisted and that's it. I lose my grip.

The strange thing is I don't feel scared. It's black, whatever's down there, as far as I can tell. I wonder how this will look? I quickly recall all the stuff that went through my head when I first woke up on the roof and this suddenly seems quite ironic. Or maybe not ironic. Just unfortunate. I don't know anymore. Alanis Morisette has me all backwards on that one.

I can't breathe.

Now I can.

I've landed on some lawn chairs. I start to stand up and I feel this sharp pain in my lower back. I'm tempted to flop back down amongst the broken lawn furniture and say, *Screw this,* and crash out until someone finds me and can piece me back together. But I don't. I look up. There's the window about eight feet above my head. I look over the balcony: about twenty-five feet down. And I feel it happening but there's nothing I can do about it. I grab my wang and try to clamp down on it—it's just reflex, even though I realize that right now I should be yanking down my shorts and whipping it out, which I start to do, but it's too late. All the beer and other toxins are just racing out of me, fueled by adrenaline. I soak the front of my shorts before I actually get the horrible hog loose and let him flood whatever's down below.

I pull my shorts and boxers off and separate them. The boxers are pretty soaked, and I'll be damned if I'm going to haul these things around with me all night. Which is a real bummer because I was rather sweet on these boxers. They're red with little white hearts, and these are the boxers I always wear them when I think I'm about to hook up with a chick for the first time.

I toss the boxers aside.

"You're not going to just leave those there are you?"

I turn and a woman is standing in the doorway behind me. She looks vaguely familiar. I say:

"Uh."

I'm at a loss for what to say next so I scratch the back of my neck and look over in the direction of the boxers like I hadn't yet made my decision as to their fate. I'm a little amazed at my fast thinking. If this had happened any other night I'd probably just be standing here looking like a dumb ass.

"Do you know you're half naked?"

Actually that hadn't crossed my mind until just this second. I'm naked from the waist down, barring, of course, the fact that

I still have my shoes and socks on. I must look like a real champion. I realize also that the sky is fading from black to violet. I can't imagine how long I was on that roof. It also occurs to me that this is Lia's mother, and that because it is a little chilly right now my penis is the size of the tip of my thumb. I hang my head, nod, and start putting my shorts back on.

"Why don't you pick those up," she points at the boxers, "and then come down to the kitchen. I'll get you a bag to put them in." She turns and goes back into the house.

This is the same feeling I used to have when I was little and mom used to take me to the dentist. I was dreading the whole ghastly ordeal for days, but it really didn't hit me until we were in the waiting room. I knew then that at any second some ample bosomed dental assistant would peak her head through the door and call my name. And there was nothing I could do to stop it. Of course, that didn't stop me from trying. I would sit there and close my eyes, and I didn't go to sleep exactly, but it was something close to that. I was aware of everything going on around me, but it felt like I was dreaming. I kept thinking that maybe if I could stay in that state forever time would stop and nothing would have to happen anymore.

I used to do the same thing sitting on the shoreline on those mornings when we would leave my grandmother's house.

The last time I tried it was right before they took mom into the operating room. I was sitting by her bedside and she was holding my hand. I closed my eyes and I could hear her and dad talking. Then dad was shaking my shoulder and mom wasn't in the room anymore.

And right now I want to close my eyes, sit down on some busted lawn furniture, forget the damp discomfort of my shorts, and not have to walk down to the kitchen with pee all over myself and drop my soiled boxers into a bag in front of Lia's mom. I've had my share of humiliation over the last few days.

I pick up my boxers with my thumb and forefinger and start thinking about what Lia said the other morning when that guy was all over me for blocking up the toilet: urine is sterile. I'd never known that. I guess not many people do because everyone gets so freaked about pee, like it's the most vile stuff since New Coke. That doesn't make me feel any better about having doused myself in it, though.

It looks as though everyone has cleared out of the house. I pass a bunch of doors that are shut, so conceivably people could be sleeping in those rooms. No one is crashed out on the floor. This has been a fairly classy affair.

Lia's mom is in the kitchen brewing coffee. I linger in the doorway. I'm unsure of the protocol in a situation where you're holding your urine soaked underwear in front of a chick's mother. She says:

"Here," and points to a large Ziplock bag lying on the counter. "I was asleep and I heard a crash. I thought maybe these drunk boys we'd thrown out at the end had come back and were smashing bottles against the house. Boys can be ridiculous sometimes. But it was you." She looks at me like it's my turn to talk, like I'm expected to explain something, and I guess, really, that I need to. I fumble with the Ziplock: it's one of the fancy ones that I've glimpsed only on commercials. It has a real zipper on it so there's no mistaking that you've closed it. Obviously, Lia's mom is a person that appreciates the finer things in life. I decide, based on her choice of food storage bags, that it would be best if I sounded as unstupid as possible.

"Well, I fell from the roof. It was rather unfortunate that your lawn furniture had to break my fall, but also it was fortunate, for I might have sustained serious injury to my person." And then, a brilliant flourish occurs to me. "I suppose that I was not unlike the character from Greek mythology who flew too close to the sun and tumbled to earth." I am most pleased with myself. English was one of the few classes I managed to stay awake in. I'm really on my game this morning. It must be the adrenaline.

She squints at me and asks:

"Why were you coming down that way? Why didn't you just come down the way you went out?

I knew I wasn't going the right way. I put my hand to my chin like I'm thinking, which I am. It now occurs to me that this was the hand I was holding my boxers with. I take the hand away, but I realize I'll be expected to talk when I do, so I put it back. However, I don't want it on my chin. Screw it:

"Look, I don't know. I don't know how I got up there. I was messed up at the time, and I got stuck by myself. I just wanted to get down and fast because there was some nut job on the roof next door hassling me."

She stares at me blankly. She must think I'm the biggest tool on the planet, and quite frankly I don't blame her. I look down at my boxers in the baggie. I'm trying to recall the best way to the front door. She snickers.

"You met Mr. Haxton. He can be a supreme prick, but he's harmless. My name is Carol. Remember?"

"Possibly?"

"I thought so."

She sticks out her hand. I look at it. I know I'm supposed to take it, but I've pissed all over myself. I say:

"I've pissed all over myself."

"I know. Shake my hand anyway. Urine is sterile."

I take her hand. She has a really firm grip for a woman and I grip back as hard as I can, but it's still not as hard as hers. She says:

"So you got left on the roof."

"Yeah," and I just nod, because like always, there's not really much more to it than what's there.

"That's your own fault."

I keep nodding and staring and the floor. Like Lia, she doesn't spare your feelings much. The coffee maker hisses that all the water has been cleared out of its insides. Carol says:

"Coffee?"

"No. I better be getting it on down the road."

"You can stay here if you like. On the couch. I have some of my husband's stuff packed away somewhere that you could change into."

I want to say yes. I'm beat to death and I would love to pass out again. However, I feel that I need to regroup:

"Nah, that's okay. Better let my folks see me for a change." I smile a little. She smiles a little. The coffee smells good. Things don't seem as awful as they did a few minutes ago.

"Did you get a chance to talk with Lia?" She asks.

"No."

"Okay. Be safe."

"I will." I turn and walk towards the front of the house. It's gotten a lot brighter outside. I carry my bagged boxers by my side trying to look nonchalant and head for Paul's place where the front door will be unlocked, and (I hope) the couch will be empty.

CHAPTER TEN

Love or Just Confusion?

I WAKE TO THE WORST cotton mouth of my life. I go to the kitchen for a glass of water and a small roach crawls out from under an empty pizza box on the counter and slips behind the dishwasher. I hate seeing things like that; it makes me all itchy when I'm trying to crash out on the couch. I let the water run for a few seconds: it always comes out with a slight brownish tint in the mornings. I suppose it can't be too bad for you. I've been drinking it for years and it doesn't seem to have done too much damage.

I go back to the couch and crawl under the blanket that Paul left out for me. All said and done, I don't feel too swift. My body aches like I'm coming down with a cold. I imagine it's a combination of the ecstasy and falling from the roof.

"What happened to you?"

Paul is standing at the bottom of the stairs, buck naked, scratching his nads. I look away to the ceiling:

"Jesus, dude, put some shorts on. I'm not going to talk to

you with your boys all out in my face."

"So did you bone her last night?"

Against my better judgment I look at Paul and fortunately for me he is sitting in the chair opposite me with a cushion covering his lap.

"No."

"What? I saw her take you by the hand and lead you off, baby. What went wrong?"

"I blew it. I mean, I don't even know if that was in her game plan, but if it was I certainly shut that one down. I passed out—and on the roof no less. She left my ass up there."

Paul laughs at me and starts grabbing at cigarette packages on the table, crumpling the empty ones, which is just about all of them. He says:

"Well, I thought you'd given it to her good. You've got scratches all over your neck."

"Christ. I fell into some lawn furniture. How am I going to explain this to Meg?"

"Fell into some lawn furniture?"

"Is she here? Or did she go home?"

"I don't think so. I came home by myself. Let me tell you: I don't know what your situation was, but I was seriously obliterated. The drug genie bent me over and made me her bitch, and the weed didn't help because I was torqued. Just flat out torqued, dude. I was sitting somewhere in the house on someone's bed, air drumming to the music because I couldn't stop moving, and one minute there were a bunch of people in there with me, and the next they're all gone. I have no recollection of them leaving. No idea where Lourdene or Craig or Megan went to. I figured you were with that girl, and I just wanted to crash, so I took off. It took me an hour to get home. I remember being in Sabastino's and trying to buy cigarettes and the bastard that I buy smokes from every day of the year wouldn't sell them to me because I didn't have my ID. Next thing I know I'm waking up in my bed, naked, and Lourdene is with me."

I wonder if Megan made it home safely? I imagine she must have, because if something had happened surely I would have heard about it by now. Besides, apparently our psychos around here wouldn't have attacked her unless she was carrying a Big Mac, so I'm pretty sure she's safe.

Suddenly it occurs to me that Lia might be at work.

"What time is it?"

"Do I look like Big Ben?"

I sit up and start kicking my shoes on. I feel like ass, like nastiness incarnate is oozing from my pores. I try to remember where I left my board last night before we took off for the party.

"What's on tap tonight?"

Paul looks at the floor like he hasn't heard me. I'm about to repeat my question and he says:

"Shit. It's Lourdene's birthday."

"Did you just now remember?"

"Yes. I guess we're all getting together here to celebrate. She's 21. Can't let that go by without somebody puking. I was thinking about going to the rave up at No Borders just for the heck of it but I guess that's out."

"Solid. I'll be in touch."

I go get my board out of the kitchen as Paul tromps back up the stairs. As I'm about to shut the door I hear:

"Happy birthday, baby!"

"Go fuck yourself, Paul!"

I'm still not sure what time it is but the sun is high and it's hot. I make the turn onto Teall Avenue and get some good wind going. They've got the road blocked up ahead for construction so I make the jump up onto the sidewalk. I'm still foggy from sleeping so late and being so out of my head last night. But I'm in the groove with the board, whipping it around the pedestrians, navigating the space like I'm Top Gun or something. It reminds me of my younger days when I really had some skills.

Coming up on Erie Boulevard I've got the light and a clear lane. I'm crouched down low on the pavement and I whip into the A-Plus Mart lot, jumping up right before the glass windows and kicking the board with me and catching it in my right hand. Maybe I've still got some stuff after all. Hopefully, this little display of superior kung-fu will put me on the road to recovery from last night with Lia. I'm not even sure why it would, but it seems like it should count for something.

The sun is glaring against the glass and I can't see in. I go for the door, trying to think what I should say. I was a complete loser last night, falling asleep, and no doubt her mom told her what a wanker I was falling off the roof and pissing myself, then trying to leave my boxers on the balcony. I may have dug myself a hole seriously too deep this time.

"Hi. That was neat."

A girl is behind the counter who is not Lia. I say:

"You're not Lia."

She seems put off by this but keeps smiling, just not as big.

"No. She doesn't work here anymore. Where'd you learn to do that?"

I don't answer her right away. I'm trying to understand what the situation is here. I can't believe I just pulled that dismount and no one saw it.

"Do you know where she is?"

"Who?" The girl still has this pleasant look about her and it's beginning to make me uncomfortable.

"Lia. She works here. Or did."

"I know. Where'd you learn to do that? My last boyfriend had a skateboard but I don't think he ever rode it."

"Huh."

"That was really cool what you did. I mean, really. My last boyfriend never could have done something like that. He was a jerk."

"Yeah." But I don't say it like I'm interested or I don't believe her. I just say it to be saying it. I don't want to offend her and just leave, but I've got to go. I'm really dragging that Lia's not here.

I look down at today's newspaper on the counter. The headline reads: *Police Still Without a Motive for McDonald's,* and then in smaller print beneath this, *Investigation reveals shooter's past as failed professional disc golfer*. I envision parents raiding their children's rooms looking for signs of dangerously influential frisbees. Of course, recent experience has taught me that they are not entirely benign.

"I mean, he totally screwed me over for this other girl. Just one day out of the blue I go over to his place and there she is. A real jerk. Guys are like that, jerks, you know. I bet you know some real jerks, but you seem cool. You live close by?"

"Uh."

"Well, duh, you must live close by, right, cause you didn't drive. Why haven't I seen you in here before?"

A guy comes walking up to the counter and says the coffee is out. The girl says:

"I'll be right back. Wait right here," and she gives me that smile.

I don't do any such thing.

I prop my board outside the kitchen door and go inside. I hear my sister laughing down the hall, and then I hear this other voice laughing too. This is the last thing I need right now. I don't care too much for my sister's friends. Invariably I find them looking way too hip to even talk to me, and snorting in my general direction as they walk out on the porch to smoke in that way that so many girls seem to smoke: elbow propped on their leg and the cigarette between the V of their fingers, shaking their arms violently when they talk and sucking on the butt harshly when they inhale. I have the impression that Kelly is telling them what a pervert I am, that I frequently masturbate in the bathroom (which seems like an appropriate place—does she want me doing it in the kitchen? I confess I have done it in the kitchen...), and that I burned the breasts off of her Barbie Doll when I was twelve. Although I don't feel the Barbie Doll incident should count against me so long after the fact, and also it was a G.I. Joe related casualty, which now that I think about it is somehow more disturbing. What was that little imaginative play about?

I open up the refrigerator and take out a Coke. There's a plate on the middle shelf covered with aluminum foil with a post-it note stuck to it and my name written on it. I take the plate out and lift the foil to inspect the contents: tuna helper, mashed potatoes, and a roll. Mom. I set the plate on the counter next to a medical journal that dad has left laying out. I wish he wouldn't leave these things where mom could see them. Of course, she knows the score, that dad is saving up to make improvements, but I think it's really a bit much to throw it in her face like this.

My sister and her friend are laughing really loud. Normally I would take this opportunity to poke my head in Kelly's room and remind her that dad is sleeping, but I guess mom can handle that. It occurs to me, however, that I am still wearing the same shorts that I peed on earlier today. I head back to my room to get some clean clothes.

There's a knock on my door as I'm pulling some shorts and a shirt out of my dresser. I turn around and mom is standing there.

"Hi, honey."

"Hi, mom."

"Did you see the plate that I left for you?"

"Yeah, thanks. You didn't have to do that." I don't move forward. I don't want her to catch a whiff of me and think that after all these years I still wet myself.

"You know I worry about you. I always will because you're

my baby. You and your sister."

"I know mom."

I stand at my dresser, shorts and shirt held low to cover any stain. I am suddenly grateful that Lia wasn't at the A-Plus; I don't think I could have handled another round of utter humiliation.

Mom makes a move out of my doorway and then turns again and comes back in the room.

"Is everything going okay? I haven't seen you much lately. I know you've got your friends, but is everything all right?"

"Yeah. Why wouldn't it be?"

"You know how I worry. I just like to know that you and Kelly can take care of yourselves."

"We can. Don't worry." As much as I often feel that mom and I need to have a little quality time this isn't the most opportune moment for it.

"Well, if anything ever happened to me or your dad..."

"Mom. Don't worry. Everything's fine. What's to worry about?"

But my mom still looks worried. I suppose all mothers are worried most of the time. I wonder why she's going on like this? I hope Kelly didn't say anything about catching me in the bathroom. My sister knowing I do that is one thing, but my mom knowing it is something else all together.

But mom's face softens, and she smiles, and crosses the room to me and puts her arms around me.

"I know you'll be okay. I just worry. You know I love you."

"I love you, too, mom."

She pulls back and looks at me, suddenly worried again:

"Does something smell like pee in here?"

"You must be imagining things."

I tried to learn the guitar when I was in tenth grade. I was going to be a rock star, groupies on my tour bus, getting the most prime weed and having month long smoke outs to the point that when I wasn't high it would feel like I was because I'd been high for so long I'd forgotten what it felt like to be straight. Someone told me that when you played the guitar it sounded better if you did it in the bathroom because there was a natural reverb. So, I'd sit in here for hours just butchering the thing. Dad eventually told me that unless I wanted him to smash it I'd better start liking the sound of my guitar in my own room. Anyway, I never learned how to play the guitar. It hurt my fingers trying to get the chords right, and no one ever taught me how to tune it. I think of my failure to become a Rock God when I'm in the shower sometimes, listening to the reverb of my feet squeaking on the bathtub's fiberglass shell.

I step out of the bathroom and head to kitchen to heat up my plate of food. I really haven't eaten anything decent in a few days, and a hot meal after my hot shower would be just the thing to heal me. From behind me I hear:

"Hey."

I turn around and it's Lia. I don't know what to say, so I say:

"Hungry?"

"No."

"Oh. Thirsty? We've got Coke and stuff. Juice."

"I'm fine. I just had a Coke with your sister."

"Oh." I want to say, *Look, you are the most beautiful girl*

I've ever seen. I can't believe you ever spoke to me, I'm sorry I passed out on your roof, I don't know why you are in my house but something about you makes me feel good. But let's face facts here: that would make me sound like a desperate idiot. Instead I say:

"Well, you don't mind if I eat, do you?"

"No."

I open up the microwave and put the plate in, set the timer and start it up. As the microwave kicks on I say to Lia:

"How'd you know where I live?"

"Found your wallet on the balcony. Must have fallen out of your shorts when you took them off," and she starts to laugh and produces my wallet from the back pocket of her jeans. I frown and take the wallet and put it in my shorts. She says:

"Cheer up, butter cup. Don't you think it's funny?" She smiles at me, and I want to melt into the floor. I've never felt this way when any girl has smiled at me, not even Megan—not even when she's about to give me a hand job and she looks up at me with those boy-are-you-going-to-love-this eyes. Of course, pride makes it impossible for me to have a rational reaction to this:

"Cheer up? Cheer up? You've got to be kidding me. You left me on the roof. I could have rolled off and killed myself, which I nearly did anyway trying to get down, though only because some fruit who lives next door wouldn't shut up about the universe—"

"Jordan."

"—so I piss myself because I'm so scared I thought I was going to die, and not only that but your mom sees me pissing myself—"

"Jordan."

"—just hold on, and to top it all off, she makes me put my soiled boxers in a Ziplock bag to carry home with me, and which I have somehow lost, so no, I don't think I can cheer up."

Lia stares at me blankly:

"Your microwave is on fire."

"Fucking fuck." Of course, the second she says it I realize what I've done: I forgot to take the aluminum foil off of the plate. I open up the microwave and smoke puffs out. I grab the edge of the plate and chuck it in the sink, turn the water on. I think I've burned the tips of my fingers. My karma is all out of whack.

Lia stands beside me looking down at the burned, wet mess of food and aluminum foil in the sink. The smoke alarm goes off. She starts to giggle, and at first I'm like, *My life sucks sweaty nads,* but then I start to giggle too.

"Goddammit!" Dad's door slams open down the hall. I grab Lia's arm and start for the door:

"Come on."

She resists for a second, then we're outside and walking down the street at a brisk pace. If I won't run from a pack of drunk and angry frat boys then I'm not running from my dad and flaming tuna helper either.

After a few blocks of walking I say:

"How long were you at my house?"

"About an hour or so."

"Sorry about that."

"It's okay. I was talking to your sister. She's cool. Too bad you two don't get along."

"She tell you that?"

"She said you two don't really have anything to talk about."

I think about this. Lia says:

"She showed me your room."

"Is that a fact." I'm trying to remember if I left something incriminating laying out but nothing really comes to mind. Still, that doesn't mean there wasn't a magazine opened to a centerfold right in the middle of the floor. It's my room so I don't think about anyone else really ever going in there. None of us goes into each other's room on any regular basis; we do better just keeping to ourselves.

"Why do you have posters all over your wall except for that one spot?"

"Oh that," and I start to explain, but I quickly realize how lame it would sound so I just keep it to myself.

"You know it's nothing really. I just couldn't think of anything else to put there I guess."

"I doubt that. What's the real reason?"

"No reason. Really."

"Okay," she says. "Okay."

We walk down Hawley Avenue, not saying anything, just walking, and I'm digging it. I don't feel like I have to say anything at all to her. I think about the way the sun is hitting the buildings and why someone doesn't pick up the trash around this town. It could really be a pretty place. We make the turn together onto Crouse Avenue and start walking up toward the university. Lia says:

"Kelly told me your mom had cancer."

"Yeah, in her breast."

"My dad had cancer, too. He died when I was eight."

I don't like it when people start in on the cancer connection. I'm not trying to be a bastard here, I mean I'm sorry her dad died, but I don't see the point of talking about it all. I just stare at the ground and keep walking.

"Were you afraid?"

"Of what?" I know exactly what she means, but it's easier to pretend.

"When your mom had cancer. Were you afraid she was going to die?"

"I guess."

"I figured that. I wasn't afraid that my dad was ever going to die. I was young, so maybe I wasn't tuned into what was going on. But he died and sometimes I think that maybe if I had been afraid he wouldn't have died. Which is ridiculous, I know. I know that has nothing to do with the fact that he died, but I can't help feeling that way. Sometimes now I'm afraid for people just so something bad doesn't happen to them. Even if there's nothing that should make me afraid. I don't know why I'm telling you this. Do you ever feel afraid that your mom will get sick again?"

"It's not like that. They cut her breast off."

"Kelly didn't tell me that."

"Yeah. Are you hungry? Because I haven't eaten since yesterday and that whole deal with what my mom cooked didn't turn out so well."

"Not really, but I can watch you eat. How does your mom

feel about the fact that she only has one breast?"

"She wears a fake thing inside her bra."

"That must be weird."

"I wouldn't know."

Lia stops walking. I take a few more steps and then I stop too. I turn and look at her. I realize I've got my teeth clenched so I try to smile a little so it doesn't show in my face. It's bad form to let a girl know so soon after you've met just how easily you can get irritated. Lia says:

"You don't want to talk about this, do you?"

"I don't much see the point. I don't like talking about cancer, or dying. I don't like thinking about it. I don't like the whole idea of it, that suddenly you cease to be. It doesn't seem fair that you have to suffer through all this and then you die. I don't like it."

Lia looks at me.

"You know, realizing your own mortality is an event you're supposed to say *yes* to."

I look past her and consider this. If saying yes to your own mortality means filling a Ford Pinto with fast food then I'm fine with living in denial.

"Let's go eat," I say.

"Okay. I understand. What are you hungry for? I could actually go for a slice of pizza now that I think about it. I'll race you to Archie's." Before I can answer she starts running.

"I'm not running."

She doesn't stop. I yell a little louder:

"I'm not running!"

I start walking the few blocks to Archie's. I hear her yell from

up ahead:
    "You suck!"
    Most days I might argue with that.

CHAPTER ELEVEN

Everything Sucks

I'M SITTING ON THE COUCH at Paul's (as always), Megan pressed against me to an uncomfortable point (as always). I tried sending a subtle message by scooting further down the couch every so often, but every time I did she slid right up against me until I'm where I'm at now: mashed against the couch arm with her crushing into me. It's made worse by the fact that I can't figure out how to tell her it's done. I mean, I'm only twenty, right? It's not like I'm going to marry Megan. We were going to break up sooner or later, just like everyone does, so it shouldn't come as any huge shock to her.

The larger problem, though, is that she's going to want to know where all of this is coming from. What can I really tell her? I met some girl at the A-Plus and everything we had has been rendered irrelevant in a matter of days? Which, of course, is precisely the case. But talk about potential for a psychotic moment. After months of begging for *it*, Megan finally let me have it. I was able to hook her like no other guy before. I'm not sure how I did it either. Sometimes I don't feel like such a good guy and I can't figure out why anyone would like me in the first place. Other times I want to be a bad guy and I fail miserably at it. The rest of the time I'm just me, and that doesn't seem to mean much at all.

But to top off the fact that I'm going to have to face an uncomfortable situation with Megan, Lara and Brenda have brought along two frat boys. They're both wearing Polo shirts and baseball caps branded with the stamp of their fraternity. What pisses me off is that I seem to be the only one who has a problem with these guys being here. Even Paul is laughing and shooting the shit with them, and after what nearly happened to us the other night. Granted, these guys are not of that clan (as best as I can tell), but they're of the same ilk.

Frat Boy #1 says:

"So you guys grow up here?"

He looks around at me and Paul and the rest of us. Paul says:

"Yeah."

"That's cool," and Frat Boy #1 just nods his head and takes a sip of his beer.

I want to tell Frat Boy #1 that no, it's not cool to be from here, that this town sucks, and that all there is to do is get wasted and work a lousy job and maybe marry a townie girl who's not completely crazy. And in-between all of that utter joy you just try and not think about how the time is oozing by towards your death. I'm sure this is a delightful little town when you're on shore leave from the world for four years, but over the course of a life it wears a bit thin. I decide to share some of these facts:

Megan cuts me off:

"So you guys like living in a house with all those other guys?"

Frat Boy #1 nods and looks at #2 who says:

"You know, it really rocks. Like, studying? Forget it. There's no way you're getting that done. Too much is going on so you have to go to the library to make the grades, but it's a real blast. Like having a house full of brothers. People get the wrong idea about Greeks on campus, like all we do is party. But it's really all about brotherhood, like real family." Numbers 1 and 2 look at one another and nod, then do a complicated little handshake.

"You girls should come to one of our mixers in the fall. It's totally awesome," F.B. #1 says.

I can't take these guys seriously with their Animal House vibe. And why does Megan care what goes on in a frat house anyway? We've lived here all of our lives, and if there's one thing we hold sacred it's the fact that we don't care what goes on at that University. (Unless, of course, the football or basketball team wins a national title, and then we're more than willing to take credit for being loyal supporters.) But outside of that it's understood that those people are just passing through, onto bigger and better things, eventually winding up at the helm of the companies that will shut down the factories here and drive another nail into the coffin of this city.

Lara says:

"That's what I always hated about not going to college: missing all that kind of stuff, like being in a sorority."

"Me too," says Megan.

You know, it's not entirely out of the realm of possibility that when I was passed out on that roof last night that I was abducted by aliens and transported to a dimension identical to my own in every way, except for subtle things, because that's the only explanation for the insanity that is unfolding before me. And also Lia showing up at my house and being terribly friendly. In fact, extraterrestrial abduction seems like the only answer at this point. I couldn't begin to tell you the number of times I've sat in a room with these very people just trashing frat boys. And not to mention the sorority girls, all dressed the same way in their tight black stretchy pants and white blouses, with those absolutely stupid shoes—the big platform jobs that make the girls walk wobbly because they're concentrating so hard on keeping their balance.

Lara is asking the Frat Brothers about formals, and Megan and Brenda are equally starry-eyed at the revelations taking place. I know this is a not-so-veiled way of Lara maneuvering herself into a position where she might get asked to one, since she'll never know the pleasure herself, having forsaken her true desire to belong to the Greek System in order to bless us with her presence.

Megan squeezes my arm and then turns to me and smiles like: *Isn't this all so exciting?* I stare at her blankly and she gives me the, *Come on—Smile!* face, then turns back to what the Frat Boys are saying after giving my arm another affectionate squeeze.

Maybe they're just being polite, but Paul and Craig look too interested in all this crap. And Craig—he even looks like he's just found the brothers he was separated from at birth. Am I the only one that finds this bizarre? I don't like these guys, and not just them, but everything they stand for. Since I was a kid all I've heard about was the basketball team and the football team, and what a good school Syracuse is, and how I should go there so that I can make phat money.

Everyone is cracking up, so I tune back in to see what terribly charming cocktail chatter #1 and #2 are laying down. They're on a roll talking about the various sadistic methods they use to abuse their pledges, putting them in a coffin, taking them into the cemetery and nonsense like that to symbolize their rebirth into the "brotherhood."

"And this pledge was so scared, like we were actually going to bury him or something, that when we helped him out of the coffin he was completely pale and had pissed himself!"

Everyone just howls but I don't even crack a smile. Megan says into my ear:

"What's wrong?"

"Nothing."

"Bullshit. You've been pissy all night. How'd your neck get scratched?"

This is the last thing I want to explain, so I say:

"I fell off a roof."

"Seriously. What's your problem?"

"Nothing, really. I just don't think that some guy getting so scared that he pisses himself is that funny. It's kind of cruel when you get down to it." I suspect I'm talking louder than I need to which is confirmed by Brenda:

"What's up your ass?" Everyone goes into hysterics again. I stand up and walk into the kitchen and out the back door to the porch. As I'm stepping outside I hear One or Two say something but I'm not sure what, and it's probably for the best. I consider cruising right off the porch and around the front of the house to the street and back home—which would mean another night of walking since my board is inside. Or maybe I could go by Lia's. Just anything else right now besides being here.

I hear someone come out the door behind me but I don't turn around. I'm doing my best to seem supremely *pissed* when in reality I'm only vaguely annoyed. However, being vaguely annoyed carries little dramatic weight with it.

"What's up, fat cat?" Paul says.

"I'm in a funk, man."

"No shit."

I turn around to make sure no one is standing just inside the doorway and when I confirm it's clear I say:

"It's Megan, dude." And as an afterthought:

"Also, those two douchebags with Brenda and Lara. Why are they even here?" I kick at an empty Molson bottle that has toppled onto its side. "But really it's Megan. You know, mostly."

Paul takes out a cigarette and offers me one. He lights them both and doesn't say anything to me. I break the silence:

"A-Plus girl came by the house this afternoon."

"Seriously? Did she come for the dick?"

"No. I wish. No, but it was cool. We talked, had some pizza. She's all right. I mean, I just think I have so much more in common with her than I do with Megan. She's something else."

We smoke our cigarettes quietly. I have a fierce urge to see

Lia. It's the greatest feeling. I can't imagine anything else in the world could make me feel this way right now except seeing her, and I've never even kissed her. Usually I need to have kissed a girl or done some titillating heavy petting to be motivated by urges of desire like this.

"So. What are you going to do?"

I give Paul a sharp look. I don't even have to think this one over:

"Hell if I know."

"Well, look, it's Lourdene's birthday. We're all just drinking, having a good time, trying to spread a little joy. Think you can keep this all under wraps for a few more hours?"

I want to say *No*, because I feel like wallowing in self-pity right now. But Paul, my best friend, is asking me for a favor.

"Yeah. I guess."

"All right, baby. That's what I like to hear."

Paul flicks the butt of his cigarette off the porch and then reaches into his shirt pocket and produces a joint.

"Here. I was saving this for a little later. Maybe it'll help you out now."

Craig comes cruising out:

"Hope I'm not keeping you girls from playing with your pussies."

Paul and I don't say anything to him. Instead, Paul fires up the joint, takes a drag, then passes it over to me. Personally, I'm not too fond of smoking from a joint: it kills my throat the next day. But it would be impolite to decline Paul's offering. I give a good, hard suck and immediately start coughing. Paul shakes his head and Craig snatches the joint from my finger.

Craig passes the joint to Paul as he blows out a long stream of smoke. Paul takes another good hit and holds it in and starts the rotation again.

I look skyward. Naturally, I can't see anything because of the streetlights. I wonder if Lia knows that Venus is at its brightest right now. If she's spent any amount of time on her roof she does.

The door opens behind Craig and I hear Megan pouting:

"You guys suck. I can't believe you're not sharing."

Paul says:

"We were getting in touch with our feelings. See? You've made me feel so vulnerable," and he runs into the apartment squealing like a little girl.

"So where is it?" Megan says.

I turn to Craig and he just kind of looks at me. He holds the joint in my direction.

"No, that's all Meg. I'm good right now."

Craig holds it out to Megan, and for a second she doesn't move to take it. Then just as she begins to reach out Craig drops it.

"People, people. What the fuck?"

They're both just standing there looking at the joint burning on the concrete floor of the porch, not making a move or anything. I reach down and pick it up and hand it to Megan. Craig says:

"Sorry."

Megan is holding the joint carefully between two fingers like she's waiting on something, like permission.

"What? Are you waiting on permission? Smoke that herb." I

hear the door open and Craig is going inside. I was hoping to avoid this being alone with Megan.

However, maybe it's the weed, but I don't feel so tense right now. I feel a lot better, like all touchy and stuff. Megan is toking on the joint and I put my arm around her and pull her close. I take the joint from her hand and get another good drag, then hand it back to her as I'm exhaling smoke. This isn't so bad. Granted, I don't feel the same electricity with Megan that I do with Lia, but who knows? That could just be the simple fact of Lia being someone different than Megan.

She hands me the last little nub of the joint and I smoke the final bit, flicking the damp roach into the yard. I look at Megan: how could I forget how pretty she really is? Certainly she's a different type of girl than Lia. I lean in to kiss her, and she kisses me back, then pulls away.

"Well someone sure is in a better mood."

I smile and kiss her again. She opens her mouth and I slide my tongue in and feel it mingling with hers. Which, of course, immediately has me rising to the occasion. I'm not wearing any underwear under my shorts. I started digging that free feeling this afternoon and wanted to see what it was like when it was done by choice. Megan slides her hands down to my ass and grabs it and pulls me against her. She laughs at my obvious excitement, then starts kissing my neck. I squeeze her tight and she lets her left hand drift away from my ass and around front, rubbing me through my shorts.

"Oh my," she says. She pulls away and looks at me, seriously, as though I've done something terribly wrong. Out of reflex I put on my best innocent face:

"What?"

She doesn't say anything, but backs up and opens the door to the kitchen and turns off the porch light that has been drawing moths and mosquitoes to it. In the sudden wash of darkness I can only make out her silhouette as she comes walking back to me, and only when her face is just inches from mine can I see how she is not smiling and yet not really frowning either. It's as if with the lights out I can suddenly see the face that was beneath the face she wore while we were kissing.

"I'm so wet right now. Do you know that?"

"I didn't know that."

"Why don't you find out?"

If this were a movie I'd be laughing myself senseless.

Megan lets her eyes drop and I look down: she is stepping right out of her shorts. She's not wearing any underwear either. What are the odds of that?

She reaches out and takes my hand and presses it against the silky coarse hair between her legs. Normally I would be tensing up right now at the prospect of dealing with Megan's seduction which will undoubtedly prove false, but with the weed, and the beer, it feels different. New.

"I want to fuck you right now," she says.

"Okay."

She takes me by the hand and has me sit on one of Paul's plastic tri-fold lounge chairs—one of those chairs that you might take to a beach or little league game. I am bewildered by all of this. Our normal modus operandi is to take advantage of secure seclusion so that we can take our time and ease things along. This is just out of control. Someone could walk out here at any minute, and I've never been one of those people who find some strange thrill in risk. I've managed to construct my whole life on the avoidance of risk, and if I were going to choose a time to upset the delicate structure I've designed this certainly wouldn't be it.

Megan keeps her eyes on mine, and she gets down on her knees in front of me and unties my Converses. She pulls them off, then pulls my socks off. She's a big no-socks person. One time when we were fooling around I forgot and left mine on. I was down between her legs, doing my best, while she lay there motionless. This was usually the norm, but for once her corpse-like demeanor seemed especially genuine and I said, *Is everything okay?* And she says, *I just can't be aroused by a man in tube socks.*

She runs her hands up my legs, up the insides of my thighs and up into my shorts. She's looking up at me, smiling slightly. She takes her hands out of my shorts, lifts herself and straddles me, taking off her shirt in the process. She grabs my head in her hands and presses her lips to mine. I take my hands and squeeze her ass, and she kisses my face and ears. I try not to think about how this is going to end up. I try not to think about getting caught. *Relax. Enjoy.* She lets her lips brush my ear and says:

"Fuck me."

I lean back so I can look at her.

Megan keeps her eyes locked with mine as she reaches down and begins the process of undoing my shorts. I lift my ass up so she can slip them off of me, and when she's gotten them off she resumes her position straddling me. She doesn't lean in to kiss me as I expected her to do, but instead reaches down between her legs and grips the old hog that's poking around down there. Instinctively, I try to mount a retreat to prevent her cries of pain, but she slides onto me without a word.

I close my eyes. I feel a surge of panic because I realize that I am, in fact, in a parallel universe and that the mirror-me will be back at any moment thus returning me to my true life.

I open my eyes. Megan isn't moving or anything, just sitting there biting her lower lip. Alas I'm not in another universe after all. I've been through this routine enough to know when the sex is being shut down. I pull my hips back as much as I can to start sliding out of her. Really: why wait for her inevitable plea for me to take it out? And as she usually adds: *fast*.

But as I'm pulling back she grabs my arms hard, her nails digging into me. I look at her. She still has her eyes closed, but says:

"Don't you dare," and she starts moving up and down on me, slowly, like she's getting the feel for it, and then a little faster. I'm not doing anything. I'm in such utter awe of the strange turn of events that I can do nothing but watch her face looking for some revelation of the truth.

She opens her eyes and gives me the biggest smile and then leans in to kiss me. Her tongue part my lips; I wrap my arms around her and pull her close. She pulls back and grabs my head and presses it to her breasts, and I make some attempt at trying to stimulate them, but it's really hard to do that to breasts with any sort of finesse when they're bouncing up and down in front of you. Suddenly she says:

"Oh baby. That's it. Mmmmm."

This is a new one on me. I have grown accustomed to total silence from Megan in all my sexual endeavors, the exception being when she alerts me to her discomfort. Heavy breathing will occasionally break the silence during some of the more magic moments with my tongue. She whispers in my ear:

"Do you like the way I feel?"

I grunt.

"I want to taste myself on you. Would you like that?"

I try to respond, some word or sound, but all of this is too much. I manage to nod. She raises from me and climbs down between my legs.

This is positively phenomenal. As long as she doesn't stop this phase of the experiment can end and we can explore other things. I reach down and put my hands on the back of her head. Granted, from what I've heard from women, this is fairly bad etiquette. As I understand it, since the girl is performing a service on you out of the goodness of her heart, you're supposed to just have faith that she knows what she's doing. But in my experience most girls don't know what they're doing so I'm not leaving this up to chance. I thread my fingers through her hair and grip her head tight. She stops. No, no, no.

"I told you I didn't like that."

"Sorry. I'm just so close."

I take my hands off the back of her head and she goes back to work. I've lost some momentum, but it's nothing that can't be regained. I can't believe I was so stupid to put my hands on the back of her head when I know she doesn't like it. What was

I thinking?

Come to think of it, I didn't know. And as much as I hate to do it, I reach down and put my hands on the back of her head and lift her off of me. She goes:

"What are you doing? I thought you were about to finish?"

"I am. But it's just that you never told me you didn't like my hands on the back of your head when you were doing this."

"Oh. I probably meant to. Or maybe I was thinking I told you, when really I told someone else. I'm sorry, what does it matter? Do we have to discuss this right now?"

Normally, I would see the rationale behind her question, but the fact that I've been potentially confused with an ex-boyfriend in the heat of passion really irks me. I say:

"What do you mean you've confused me with someone else?"

Which, in the retrospect of a split second, was probably not the best thing to say.

Megan looks me dead in the eye.

"No, it's not like that at all. I love you so much. I'm sorry."

"No, I'm sorry. I shouldn't have said that. It's okay."

"Really, baby, I'm sorry. You know I am. You don't know how much I love you. I love you more than I've ever loved anyone. I'd do anything for you. Sometimes I don't think you understand that," she says.

"Meg, really, it's okay."

"It's not okay. You're always moping around, and you're always so bitter or angry and I know a lot of it has to do with me because we don't have the best sex, and I just want to make you happy."

Every cell in my body tells me that if ever there was a time to start back peddling and taking the blame for something this is it:

"Meg, you make me happy, it's just—"

"Craig told me."

Every cell in my body tells me that if ever there was a moment to call a time out this is it.

"Craig told you what?" She doesn't say anything, but starts sniffling. "Craig told you what?"

"That you weren't happy with me."

"I never said I was unhappy with you."

"He said you weren't happy with trying to have sex with me, and that you just wished someone else could do it."

"I—" I stop. I don't know how to respond to that. Yeah, I said it, and I meant it, too. But Craig had no right. No right at all.

"When did Craig tell you this?"

"Last night when we were all rolling at that party."

"Look, Meg, Craig was wasted. He took something I said out of context."

She looks up at me from between my legs where she is crying, my penis still gripped tightly in her hand.

"Did you say that you wished someone else would just screw me and get it over with so there wouldn't be so much pressure on you?"

I don't want to own up to saying that. But I'm kind of buzzing here and I can't think of a good lie.

"Yes."

"I'm sorry, Jordan. Craig and I were rolling, and I only wanted to make you happy, and at the time it seemed like the thing that would make you happy, and I did it for you so you wouldn't have to do it."

Many things are bothering me right now. Suddenly I don't feel stoned, and yet I don't feel completely straight. This doesn't seem real. I feel like I've been kicked in the stomach. But the thing that is bothering me most is that Megan still has a grip on my wang. I mean, a serious grip. Discomfort to the tenth power. I say:

"Megan. Take your hand off of my penis. Please."

She doesn't let go. I'm not prepared for an emotional scene where I have to call Paul out here to help free my member.

"Megan. Let it go. Gently."

She releases me and I stand up and start looking for my shorts.

"What are you doing? Are you leaving?"

I don't say anything. And not because I don't have some pretty choice words for her, but because I just don't have it in me to deal with her right now. I discover my shorts and slip them on. Megan says:

"Jordan, I'm sorry. I didn't mean to hurt you. I did it for you. Please don't be mad. I mean, I know you'll be mad, but try to understand we were messed up and I thought this would make you happy. Be mad if you have to but just stay. Please don't go."

I turn around and look at her. I open my mouth and I hear the door open behind me.

"Hey, what are you two up to out here? Oh."

I look over my shoulder. Paul is standing there wide-eyed, at Megan I guess, who is still naked. I turn to Megan. Tears are rolling down her face. Paul says:

"What's up?"

I reach down for my shoes, decide I can live without socks, and push past Paul into the kitchen. Megan shouts my name.

Brenda looks up as I walk into the living room. She blows a stream of smoke out of her mouth and says:

"Hey, all done hot shot? What are you? The minute man?"

Everyone bursts out laughing.

"Shut up, Brenda."

"Hey dude, it's all good. Have a toke on this." Frat Boy #1 is holding his bowl out to me. I don't need a confrontation with this ape, so I demonstrate some restraint:

"Blow me." I grab my board from beside the door and walk out to the street. I hear someone inside say something that I can't make out, and then an outburst of laughter. Bastards.

I sit down on the curb and start to put my shoes on. The reality of everything is starting to hit me. I feel hurt, and betrayed, and all of it puts me on the verge of vomiting. Which I keep a lid on. I don't want the people inside to hear me retching and think I've gone soft.

I hear the front door open. I can't deal with any more drama right now. I decide to tie my other shoe when I can do it without interruption. I hop up, put one foot on the board and get it going with the other. I get about three good kicks in when I'm suddenly flat on my face.

Asphalt smells a certain way in warm weather that it doesn't any other time of the year. I suppose it has to do with the heat beating down on it all day; it makes the tar come alive, so that whenever I smell it I think of being in the car with my dad when I was little and we were stuck on the highway for the longest time. We didn't have air conditioning in the car and it was so miserably hot. I don't think dad and I really said much the whole time we sat in traffic, but I remember at some point saying, *Jesus dad, I wish we could just move*. He nodded and said, *Boy, that's about the best wish you could have*. It was one of the few moments in my life where it felt like my dad and I actually connected. Too bad I had to use that moment up when I was seven.

Since that occasion in the car with dad, the smell of tar always makes me think of roads yet to be traveled and beckoning to me. The street I'm on now is connected to another street. And that street connects to another one, and so on, and it never ends, stretching out across the country as one big sea of asphalt into parking lots and driveways and highways. Anywhere has to be better than Syracuse. I'm puzzled as to why I've never taken Paul seriously. The ease of it all never occurred to me. It's simply a matter of going straight for a while, then making a turn, then another, and suddenly you will have arrived in a place wholly other to you.

But I've got bigger problems in the here and now. My shoelace is tangled in the wheels of my skateboard.

"Are you okay?" Paul is beside me and I feel his hands on me, turning me over. I lie on my back staring up at the trees arched over the street and the darkness huddled between the branches.

"Help me up." I extend my arms to Paul and he grabs them and yanks me to my feet.

"Thanks," and take a step, which is a stupid thing to do

because I'm still tangled up in my wheel. I stumble and nearly go face first into the pavement again, but Paul catches me. He has the most concerned look, like if something is wrong with me then certainly his world is out of balance, too. It's the sweetest thing. I can't remember anyone looking at me like that in the longest time, except for my mom, but she doesn't count because that's how she's always looked at me. I can't imagine her looking any other way. I start laughing.

Paul starts laughing, too, and sometimes that's about all you can do when the cosmos is conspiring against you.

I double over. This is absolutely ridiculous. I can't remember when I've laughed so hard. Paul lets go of me and I drop to the ground and start laughing even harder. I'm not making any noise either. My eyes are watering—it's that funny.

And then suddenly it's not that funny and I start crying. Paul is still laughing, so he doesn't know what the deal is. I don't want him to know either, so I start trying to get my shoelace undone from my wheel, but it's no use. It's tangled up pretty good.

I don't even know why I'm crying. I find it hard to believe that I would be all torn to pieces about this thing with Craig and Megan. After all, I was on the verge of dumping her, so no big deal, right? This just makes things all that much easier.

And yet for some reason it's not that simple.

Paul asks:

"What's the deal, fat cat?"

I can't speak. I try to but when I open my mouth I can only produce hiccup-like gasps.

"Dude, seriously, what is it?"

I take off the shoe that's tangled up in the skateboard. I gather the board and the shoe and hold out my hand to Paul who takes it in his hands and pulls me from the ground for the second time tonight. He grabs me by the shoulders and says:

"What is it?"

But I can't look at him like this. I turn away and manage to say:

"Paul, please. Later."

Maybe it's something in my voice. He takes his hands off of my shoulders and says:

"Okay."

I didn't expect that. He's usually such a stubborn bastard. I stand still not knowing exactly what I'm going to do. And then I start down the street. I feel somewhat foolish, of course, because I'm hobbling in that peculiar manner that naturally occurs when you've only got one shoe on. Paul calls out:

"Don't do anything stupid."

I almost start laughing again.

One of these days I might actually invest in a watch so I can tell people just how long I've been sitting around. As it stands right now I can't begin to guess the span of time I've been sitting across the street from Lia's considering whether or not I should go and knock on her door or just go home. Or neither.

But I don't have many options unless I get my shoe loose from my board. In my attempts at freeing it I somehow have only managed to make it worse. I ultimately tried rubbing the shoestring on the edge of the curb to break it, but that didn't seem to do much either. Going forward I will be suspect of any movie or TV show in which someone frees himself from captivity by rubbing a thick piece of rope on the edge of a stone.

A guy is walking down the sidewalk on the opposite side of the street, which is fine, except for the fact that he crosses onto my side as soon as he sees me. I don't feel like being screwed with right now. That's another thing about Syracuse: it snows from October through April, and because you can really only hang outside for five months out of the year, the crazies have to put a little extra effort into hassling you. I act as though I'm not paying much attention to him, but not as if I don't notice him because that would make me an easy target for a mugging. It occurs to me, though, that I don't have any money anyway.

He stops directly behind me and I turn my head so I can see him out of the corner of my eye:

"Hey man, didn't we go to school together?"

I hope not. I hate running into people I went to school with. I say:

"Maybe. Where'd you go?

"Where'd you go?"

"Central."

"Hey, that's where I went."

"Is that a fact."

It occurs to me that the best course of action might be for me to get up and go over to Lia's. But I've been through this kind of thing before. I wouldn't put it past this guy to follow me over there and get Lia tangled up in this. He's a real talker; I can tell. Despite the fact that we apparently share an alumni bond he makes no move to come around where I can clearly see him.

He says:

"What's your name man?"

"Dick."

"Yeah, man, Dick, that's right. I remember you. I'm Marcus. You remember me, right? We had trigonometry together."

The Universe has a funny way of humoring itself. I say:

"No."

"Huh?"

"No. No I don't."

"You don't what?"

"Know you."

"Come on, man. You know me. We went to school together."

I hate these guys. They always have to make a big production about hitting you up for some change. Which, in a way, I guess is okay because it makes you feel as though you're paying for a brief bit of street theater. However, I wish this guy would just cut to the chase.

"Look, I don't have any money."

"Bitch, what do I look like to you? Do I look like I need money? Do I look fucking homeless?"

"I don't know what you look like."

I had a feeling things were going to end up like this, but my day has been ruined as it is, so I just shrug my shoulders.

"Is that all you got to say *bitch*? No one talks to me like that," and I hear something click behind me. I can't tell if it's a gun or a knife. I'm hoping for a gun, because if I'm going to die I want it to be quick. But with my luck it's a knife, and he probably won't even kill me. I'll be brutally paralyzed from the waist down and rendered incapable of getting a boner. The guy says:

"You want me to cut you?"

Well, that answers that. I say:

"Yeah, but if you're going to do it, make sure you're not half-assed about it."

I wait for something—for him to say something or to stab me.

"What's up with your board?"

I jump a little, startled by the sound of his voice.

"Got my shoe caught in it."

"How the fuck did you do that?"

"Shoe was untied. I hopped on in a hurry. You know."

"Why didn't you take the time to tie your shoe? You could bust your ass doing something like that."

"I did, but whatever."

"What?"

"My girlfriend told me about an hour or so ago that she banged a friend of mine. She was giving me head at the time."

"Shit."

"Yeah."

I nod my head, and I get the impression that the guy behind me is doing the same thing, but I'm still a little too sketched out to verify this.

"Bitches. Fucking bitches man. What you going to do? Can't do a Goddammed thing. It's all about that pussy, know what I'm saying?"

"Yeah."

"That the bitches house over there you been looking at?"

"No, that's another girl."

"Right on. My boy got it going on. That's the way you got to be. One bitch, man—one bitch with many faces."

I'm not sure how to respond so I don't.

"Give me your board, man."

"What?"

"Give me your fucking board."

I think about protesting but I can't seem to muster up the energy. I hand it over silently. He hands it back to me almost immediately, minus the shoe, which he tosses in my lap.

"There," he says. "Now you won't look like such a fool when you go to the door."

"Thanks."

"It's cool man. Now go hit that shit."

I hear him start off, and I turn to finally get a good solid look at the guy but it's as if he fades right into the shadows. It's twisted. Sliding my shoe back on a name flashes in my mind and I call out:

"Marcus Ford!"

He voices comes out of the dark; I'm not sure from where:

"What?"

"We had trigonometry together!"

"I know that!"

I want to tell him that my name isn't Dick, but I guess he knows that, too.

CHAPTER TWELVE

Don't Change Your Plans

"Was that you yelling out here?"

I'm on Lia's front porch, board tucked under my arm. I was hoping for a little fanfare at my arrival. You know, a sort of boys-home-from-the-war kind of thing, but no such luck. It seems like no one ever greets me with the response to which I feel I'm entitled. I don't answer her about the yelling but instead say:

"Hey, I was just in the neighborhood, you know, thought I'd stop by and see what you were up to."

She gives me a disbelieving look.

"What happened to that thing at your friend's place?"

"Ah, it was lame. I didn't feel much like being there and I'd rather hang with you anyway."

She smiles at me, but in that the way that people often smile at me when they are amused by my obvious bullshit.

Once inside we go into the kitchen. Lia's mom is seated at the kitchen table upon which rests the most massive assemblage of Legos I've ever seen. Or even imagined. It's at least three feet tall, consuming the entirety of the table, which is fairly large. A family of six could eat quite comfortably at it with room to spare. And this construction that they have produced is like a Metropolis, only in miniature. Lia's mom says:

"I can't get it. You're going to have to get it. I can't believe I didn't think of this before I built up around it. I don't know where my head was."

"We can always take down a few levels to get it in."

"No, I'm not going back. We'll just have to get it this way or forget about it. But trust me—next time I won't make this kind of mistake."

I've never wanted to know anything so badly in my life:

"What?"

Carol looks at me as if she can't quite place me.

"I forgot to put a window in the bosses' office so she can watch everyone. Like any good authority figure. It's nerve wracking to fix things once you've built around them."

"Oh," I say. "Can I look?"

"Sure. You can help if you want."

I got my first set of Legos for Christmas when I was six. It was a space outpost model which came with a single, gray square Lego platform designed to look like the surface of the moon. I can't remember anything else I got that Christmas, with the exception of a Viewmaster, which came with a series of slides of Dracula and Frankenstein that traumatized me until the following summer. Regardless, I spent the whole day building with those Legos. At some point after we had eaten dinner dad even got down on the floor and played Legos with me. I can remember him doing that only one other time when I got a race track for Christmas a few years later. After that dad didn't leave the recliner on holidays unless it involved food going into or coming out of him.

That was also the only time I received a large Lego set as a gift. When I was being bribed to go to the dentist, or on my birthday, I would get a smaller set: a race car or a small plane, something that any half-wit could assemble in under ten minutes without giving a second thought to the step-by-step instructions. Eventually I started taking all the pieces I had collected and building my own things, usually whenever I was sick or feeling bitter towards the world. It was an incredibly soothing thing to do.

Unfortunately, the Legos went the way of so many things I got for Christmas as a kid: in a series of garage sales my folks had shortly after mom got out of the hospital. Dad's paycheck was being eaten up by the medical bills, even with mom's high quality insurance through the university. Mom wasn't working for a time while she recovered, and dad was having to pull cash out of his ass to keep us going. Which he did, several times, with a garage sale. I saved the Legos the first time around, but when items for the second sale were being gathered dad gave me a huge guilt trip about not contributing to the welfare of the family. I told him he should sell the TV. He started to yank off his belt and I decided I could part with the Legos.

But I ignore Carol's invitation to help for the simple reason that I know when I'm out of my league.

The setup they have is amazing. It must have taken them

years to acquire the pieces to construct this city. It has streets lined with shops, skyscrapers, cars and people. Even the insides of the buildings are highly detailed: office spaces, hallways and stairs. It's another world that you wouldn't know about unless you peered through one of the windows. I've never come close to seeing anything like this in my life except for one of those massive Lego displays in the mall, and that took the Lego people weeks to build; it said so on the little placard in front of the exhibit. I've no idea how long Lia and her mother have been working on this since I have absolutely no memory of it just twenty-four hours ago. I look at Lia and her mom:

"This is the greatest thing I've ever seen in my life." Which isn't true. Seeing my mom after her surgery was probably the best, but this is pretty close.

Lia and her mom look at me and they both shake their heads. Lia says:

"You know you're bleeding, right?"

Actually, I didn't, but it makes sense. Personal injury has been the last thing on my mind in the last hour or so, all things considered. I look down at my knees: they've each got a nice scrape and a trickle of dried blood running down to my shins. My arms look a little cut up as well, but my legs took the worst of it. Of course, the second that Lia points out that I've taken a little damage things start to hurt. Funny how that works. I say to Lia:

"Why didn't you say something when you answered the door?"

"You looked like you needed to come in more than anything

else."

"Oh."

Carol says:

"Take him in the bathroom and throw some hydrogen peroxide on those cuts," but she doesn't divert her gaze from the Lego Metropolis.

I follow Lia into the bathroom. I sit on the toilet while she opens the medicine cabinet and starts taking out first-aid supplies. I say:

"Your mom seems pretty intense with the Legos."

"It's a serious hobby with her. We used to do it on a smaller scale when I was little, before my dad died. But since then it's gotten out of control. Mom thinks it stimulates the serotonin in the brain and helps with creativity. I think it just relaxes her as an alternative to taking some sort of pill that would do the same job."

I nod.

"Is your mom like, a hippie, or something?"

Lia laughs and shakes her head at me. She pours some hydrogen peroxide onto a cotton ball and starts dabbing at my knee.

"No. She's too young to be a genuine hippie anyway."

I feel in a daze. There is something distinctly hypnotic about her hands on my skin, the way she's so tender about everything. I could sit here for hours with her running her hands over my skin like this. It's so sensual.. And I always thought that word pretty much meant sexual, but classy sex, right? It isn't that at all. I understand that now.

"You want something on these, or should I just leave them

uncovered?"

"Whatever you think is best."

"Okay." She doesn't make a move to get a Band-Aid. Neither one of us speaks. I feel completely at ease. I expect it to be awkward but it isn't. It is so effortless to not say anything to her. Those awful silences that people usually want to fill with mindless chatter don't exist with this girl. Could this really be the same person who handed me a plunger and told me to *make sure it goes down this time*?

Lia starts moving toward my face, not taking her eyes off of mine. This is it. This is what I've been waiting for since I first saw her step out from behind the food warmers at the A-Plus Mart.

Her face is so close to mine. So close that if I wanted to see her clearly I would have to pull back a bit because she is at the point of closeness where focus falls apart. But I don't want to move my eyes from her. This is serious. I want to get it right.

Lia tilts her head to the side, so I tilt mine the other way and figure that maybe now I should close my eyes. I used to kiss with my eyes open when I was thirteen or fourteen. I discovered quickly that girls become tremendously sketched out by that.

Just as I'm closing my eyes Lia's head makes a quick movement and I feel her lips on my forehead. When I have my eyes fully open again I see her standing back and looking at me. She says:

"All done. You're as good as new now."

I blink at her.

"Come on. I have something that will make you feel a lot

better." She gives my arm a good tug and suddenly we are out in the hallway headed back towards the kitchen. Lia says:

"Mom, we're going upstairs."

"Okay."

I look into the kitchen as we pass—Carol is lost in the splendor of her creation.

I follow Lia up the stairs in silence. She doesn't let go of my hand and I like that.

Her room is dimly lit, mainly by a lava lamp and another lamp which has a small tapestry/large bandana/paisley patterned thing draped over the shade which casts strange shadows on the wall. Surprisingly, though, her room isn't what I expect. Based on my first impression of her that day in the A-Plus mart I expected a more industrial feel to her room, posters of Nine Inch Nails, stuff like that. And since then I would have anticipated a love-mother-earth-girl vibe to the place, but the decor doesn't jive with either of my assumptions. It's very girlie, all Strawberry Shortcake and Barbie Dream House. With, of course, the exception of the lighting. On the wall she has pictures of teen idols cut from magazines. It's rather confusing. She parks me on the bed.

"You're about to freak, aren't you?"

The sickly sweet aroma of posh feminine scents washes over me. I scan the room and spot a large collection of perfume bottles on the dresser. Girls as cool as her don't have cosmetics in quantity. I've been duped.

"Who exactly are you?"

"Look, I don't go bringing just any guy up here for this very reason. They all flip because my room isn't what they expected, and it tells them a little something about me that they don't like, or that they can't deal with, which is that I have a shallow streak in me. So what? If I was smart the minute your sister showed me your room I would have left your house screaming. But I didn't do that. People are complex. People are confusing. I know this."

"True."

"Besides, we all have our shallow sides. Some people like to display theirs in public. I like to keep mine just for me because it turns my stomach."

She sits on the bed next to me, wide-eyed and shaking her head, and I start to laugh because it seems like something I would do. She starts to laugh, too, and then she says:

"What's the one thing in the world that you most want to know?"

"What kind of question is that?"

"Just answer it."

I scrunch my face up like I'm thinking real hard. Some people have commented, however, that when I look this way it appears as though I am passing gas so I try to relax. I'm wondering what I do want to know most. I mean, there's a whole series of things I've been curious about. Like porn actors when they're having sex—are they really thinking about having sex, or is it just so commonplace to them that they're wondering what they need from the grocery store? But that's just one thing. I suppose I also wonder about how my parents met, if they ever thought their lives were going to turn out like this, and if they ever wanted something more. Were they headed towards a different bright spot on the horizon when I was born? I can't imagine anyone wanting the lives that they have, but so many people seem to have those same lives. And I wonder what's going to happen to me, because I don't know. I also wonder what happened to my *G.I. Joe* comic with the Zen master story in it. I look at Lia:

"Well, what about you?"

She doesn't even take a second to think about it:

"I want to know what goes on inside the head of a baby."

"Why would you want to know that?"

"Because aren't babies the weirdest thing? What's your first memory?"

I shut my eyes. I've thought about this before. I usually can recall most stuff starting from five, but before that things are really fractured.

"I'm two or three. I remember my folks giving me a bath one afternoon. The bathroom was painted blue and I can recall how the sun lit the room up and made it seem warm and safe."

"See? That's just it. You can't remember anything before that. Few people do. As a baby you're conscious, things are going on, you respond to them, but no one can remember. It's like this unknowable thing, like some part of your life you're not really certain about, and yet the stuff that happens to you when you're an infant affects who you become. If you could know what went on inside the head of a baby you might be able to make its life turn out for the better. Maybe that guy wouldn't have shot up the McDonald's if we could have looked into his head as a baby. We could have seen the anger or the craziness there and stopped it. Or maybe when we're born, we're reincarnated, like what the Buddhists believe. And those first few months or years of our lives are the shedding of all our knowledge from a past life. I just think that's the big mystery that has to be solved before anything else. When that gets solved, when we understand a baby's brain, everything else will be cake."

She stops and looks at me. "So?"

"So what?"

"What do you want to know?"

"Oh. I guess, right now, I want to know if my mom and dad still love each other."

Maybe that makes me sound like a sap, and if it does, well, forget *you*. Most of my friends' parents are divorced. They know the answer. But my family feels like it's been in limbo since mom had cancer. It didn't feel like that initially when she was declared cured—we were all so happy and lovey-dovey and my sister and I were helping out around the house. But looking back on it now I can see that there was a deep chasm opening between mom and dad. When mom was well enough to go back to work it was like they stopped talking altogether, except when it came to the most routine exchanges that were required to keep the house running.

Lia is looking at me like she's trying to see the wheels turning in my head. I'm not up for a real soul-searching moment. I smile.

"Close your eyes," she says.

If she asks me to start visualizing my happy place, hot chick or not, I'm out of here. I'll tuck my worthless skateboard under my arm and walk it home because this New Age nonsense just doesn't wash.

"Why?"

"Just do it."

I close my eyes. I feel the bed give a little as she stands, and then it seems like she's on the floor, and sure enough I can feel her hair brushing against my legs. I knew that getting sentimental about one's home life could make a woman feel pity and yield some extra action but please: I didn't even get so far as to say, *I don't want to talk about this anymore.*

But it occurs to me that it wasn't that long ago that I was inside of Megan.

"What are you doing?" Her hair brushes against my legs again and then her hands are on my thighs.

"Sit still," she says. "Be patient."

"Look, I don't know what you're getting ready to do, but if you're doing what I think you're doing you'd better stop, because I don't think it's such a good idea."

"What do you think I'm getting ready to do?"

"Well, you know... I mean, you're down on the floor in front of me."

"Jordan, open your eyes".

Lia is on her knees in front of me. She's smiling, and holding what appears to be a rolled up poster in her hands. I feel my face going red. I nod and lower my eyes.

"Well, take it."

I take the poster from her hands and hold it, admiring its beautiful tubular-ness. I can't believe I thought she was going to blow me. I'm obviously dealing with a classy chick here.

"Aren't you going to open it?"

"Oh, right."

At first it looks as though it might be one of those stupid posters involving drinking, something with an idiotic slogan like, *Tequila Crossing,* and a yellow road sign depicting a pedestrian crawling across a street. But instead it's the greatest thing that anyone has ever given me.

Lia, unknowingly, has finished my Zen rock garden. I'm holding a poster of the cover of the most recent Descendents' album. The simple line drawing depicts the lead singer, Milo, squatting on a toilet that's overflowing while reading a newspaper which has *Everything Sucks* emblazoned on the front page. Perfect.

"You like it?"

"It's the best thing that anyone has ever given me."

"You've led a really sheltered life, haven't you?" She smiles. I say:

"How did you know?" And then: "About the poster. Not my life."

"Well, I figured something was going on with all those posters in your room, and then that one blank space. I mean, come on. And I saw all those Descendents tapes on the floor. But it was just chance that I was in Down Under Leather, looking for a new bag, and they had this poster and I immediately thought of you. It says so much about you. And how we met." She starts to laugh and I start laughing too. All things considered, I suddenly feel like my life couldn't get much better right now. Sure, Megan cheated on me with Craig. Big deal. And granted, my ass has caused me nothing but shame and embarrassment the past couple of days. But everything seems to have turned out okay.

Lia sits down next to me on the bed. I look over at her. She looks at me. I want to kiss her so badly. I look away from her and lean back on my elbows.

"So."

"So," she says, and suddenly there is this tension.

I can feel it. Something is supposed to be happening but I'm not sure what. The silence isn't so cool anymore because it's happening in the place of this other thing and it's all wrong. I try to fix it. I say:

"Sorry I passed out on the roof. I was really torn up. Otherwise, you know, I wouldn't have done that.'

"It's all good. I'm sorry I left you up there. You could have gotten hurt. I wasn't thinking so straight myself."

"It's okay. I didn't get hurt. I mean, you know, not really."

I can't help myself. I lean in for the kiss. She leans toward me.

Whenever I've kissed someone for the first time it always has a certain quality to it. Not unlike, I've always thought, how the first European explorers who went west to make maps must have felt. It's like all day you've been climbing this hill, or mountain, or *plateau*, and you're just absolutely beat, just on the verge of throwing up your hands and saying, *Okay, fuck it —everyone turn around!* But you go ahead anyway, and you cross the peak just as the sun is setting, and suddenly there you are looking out at this perfect new place you've never been with this gorgeous sunset. The world has become a Goddamned Bob Ross painting.

But all the maps have been made and people are everywhere now. And sure: when the family went up to Lake Ontario I felt this way, that I had come upon unspoiled earth. But a body of water that big tends to overwhelm you, and never having seen the ocean I can't begin to speculate what that's like, or what it was to be some mountain man wearing beaver fur and hauling a musket, looking out over thousands of miles of prime earth without a single person around for thousands of miles more.

So that's how I feel whenever I touch my lips to strange lips for the first time. I mean, even more so than the first time I have sex with someone, because you really just build to sex. You've been exploring each other's body by the time you get around to doing it, so there's not that much that's new. Kissing is the toughest there is—it's like breaking the sound barrier. You're crossing into someone's personal space for the first time and you never know what could go wrong.

The best kisser I ever knew was one of the first girls I ever made out with. In high school, not long after the incident with the pig when everyone was snickering behind my back in the halls, a girl who was a senior asked me if I wanted to go to a movie with her. Maybe that doesn't sound like too much, but this wasn't just any girl, this was *the girl*.

Which doesn't explain why she would ask me to go to a movie. Besides the fact that I had a conniption over a dead pig in biology I was a tremendous dork. The best I've been able to figure out is that perhaps *the girl* felt a little pity for me. By the time she got around to asking me out it was common knowledge that my mom had cancer, and I'm sure nothing will influence a girl more than one's potential to soon be orphaned.

And to top things off her name was Barbie. And she had the most exquisitely large breasts, and blond hair that hung down to the middle of her back. (Though I've since learned from an acquaintance that it was not her natural color.)

But none of that really matters. I mean, after a date where I was essentially a dildo (I was trying to be much cooler than I actually was since I'd never been on a real date), I sat awkwardly in her Chevy Grand Prix in front of my parents' house. Naturally, she had to drive. And so I said something to her like, *Well, thanks*, and I started out of the car. But she reached her hand out and touched my cheek and I turned and she kissed me, mouth open, and her tongue went straight into my mouth. It was a completely magical moment, I mean, totally a Patrick Dempsey film. It couldn't have lasted more than ten seconds. Then I stepped out of the car and that was it. She said hi to me in the hallways at school but we never went out again.

Up until now I recall that as being the best kiss I've ever had. And it probably wasn't, it just seemed better under the circumstances. But this kiss is by far the best. Lia has the softest lips, and she seems to know exactly how to press them against mine.

Lia pulls back. I look at her and smile. She smiles too, but it's not a good one. She says:

"We can't do this."

A voice in my head says, *Play it cool, play it cool.*

She looks away and lets out a sigh.

"Do you remember what I asked you on the roof last night?"

I hate questions like this because they fall into that category of '*Do you know what day we started dating?*' and '*Do you remember what song was playing when we did it for the first time?'*

So when questions like these get thrown my way I've learned the best strategy for dealing with them is to just look at the person who's asking and blink at them, blank faced, like you're not entirely sure what they're talking about. Lia says to me:

"Of course you don't remember. You were wrecked."

I open my mouth to try and mount some defense of myself but she's right. She says:

"I asked you what you were afraid of. And you said you were afraid of dying."

I do vaguely recall something to that effect being said right before I fell asleep, but everything prior to waking up on that roof is foggy. I can't believe I actually said that, though. Usually that would be the last thing I'd admit to being afraid of. Spiders usually top my list. Death isn't something I care to discuss, but I guess I was wasted enough not to care what I said. So I say to Lia:

"What's your point?"

"And I told you that I was afraid of ski lifts in summer."

"Yeah. You did. Because I remember thinking about ski lifts right before I passed out. That really puzzled me." I nod my head, relieved to discover the source of that conjured image. Then it occurs to me:

"Why are you afraid of ski lifts in the summer?" I sound vaguely accusatory. I reach out and touch her arm and she puts her hand on mine:

"Maybe afraid isn't the right word. There's just something sad about them. You know, there are these old ski lifts down at the south end of Comstock, and when I was little I used to ride my bike up there in the summer, and there was just something terrible about them, not only because it was summer and they weren't being used, but because they had just been abandoned. It was just awful. And then, when my dad died, and I would ride my bike up there, you could hear all those rusted lifts swinging in the breeze, and it was sad, like the wailing of the dead."

I know the place she's talking about. I used to go up to those ski lifts too, and I never really found them all that sad. I just figured that whoever decided to put a ski slope on that little hill made a bad investment. There's plenty of championship slopes within an hour's drive of Syracuse. It didn't sound like the dead moaning at all to me; it sounded like rusty ski lifts and bad planning.

But, of course, I don't mention any of this to Lia. I just nod and try to come off as sympathetic as possible. I say:

"I'm sorry."

"For what?"

She's got me on that one.

"I don't know. It just seemed like the thing to say."

She nods.

"Well, ever since then, any time I saw those unused ski lifts it made me sad, and I thought about all that machinery that was meant for something and how it was going to waste. And I thought about my dad, how he was meant for me and this world, and how the cancer just wasted him and took him away. I see all these people everyday sitting on their front steps, drinking or smoking, or those clerks down at Peter's Grocery, or wherever, and they've all got the same look, like they're just stumbling through life and don't know what they're missing and I don't want to end up like that."

My stomach churns. All of this nonsense in the past couple of hours has my bowels doing strange things. I say to Lia:

"Well, if you don't want to end up like that, then don't."

"I'm not."

"Well, okay then. Seems like that's settled." I lean into kiss her, which I sense is a stupid move, but I'm just trying to steer things back to a place I feel I can manage. She pulls back:

"Are you listening?"

I try to assemble my innocent face; it's not easy on the fly.

"What?"

"I don't want to end up like everyone else in this town."

"Well, neither do I."

"That's why I'm leaving."

Not this song and dance again. As if I don't get enough of this every day from everyone else I know.

"That's good. That's never a bad plan in this city."

"I'm sorry I didn't tell you sooner."

"Well, I figured you'd leave at some point. I mean, anyone who grows up here has an escape plan."

"I'm leaving tomorrow morning. On the nine-thirty Greyhound. I'm going to live with my aunt in Asheville. In North Carolina."

"What?"

I pull my hand away from her arm. I don't know what to say. I want to look her in the eyes and tell her that she has just delivered the final blow, that this is it, that I find no reason to live. My poster garden is completed, and the girl of my dreams is leaving. I realize, of course, that I'm overreacting slightly, but I think it's appropriate.

"I mean, you know, most days I just sit around getting stoned, and just whatever, playing Nintendo, and I don't give a fuck. I was stuck with a girlfriend I didn't care about, and one day I walk into a gas station to move my bowels, and there's the most beautiful girl I've ever seen, and for once in my life I do something. I mean, I took out a rack of Twinkies for you. Do you think I just go around doing that willy-nilly? No. And you gave me the most perfect gift anyone could have ever given me and you barely know me. I'm thinking that life is turning around, like things are finally coming together, and maybe the world doesn't suck like I thought it did. But you know what? This poster you bought me is prophetic: it does suck. Everything sucks."

She reaches out and touches her hand to my cheek. She wipes something away. A tear. I didn't realize I had started crying. Twice in one night. I try to turn away but I can't *not* look. I won't see her ever again. I want to see her as much as I can.

She kisses me. Softly, on the lips, and I close my eyes. I feel the tears start to roll out. The Learning Channel has taught me that men have something in their biology that occurs every 28 days that is akin to PMS. It must be my time of the month.

"I wish I could give you more but I just can't."

"Look, if I could stop the world from turning right now I would. If I could just press my hands to the earth as hard I could and let all these feelings in me creep out of my finger tips I believe things would stop, and we could have all the time in the world that I'd like for us to have. But I can't stop things. I wish I could. So we should try to cram all the things we can into these few hours."

That's it. I've hung it all on the line. Lia looks at me, tears hanging on the edges of her eyes. She has the sweetest look on her face, so sad, and so beautiful. She says:

"That's the biggest load of shit anyone has ever said to me. Some girls might actually be stupid enough to sleep with you for saying something so obviously ripped off from a lame 80s film, but my mom didn't raise a stupid girl. I'll give you an 'E' for effort, though. It was very cute."

I realize my mouth is hanging open. I close it, then open it and go:

"But—"

She puts her fingers to her lips.

"If I'm going to do something I don't want to waste it. I want it to be as sweet as it could be, and we couldn't do that. It would be rushed, and wrong, and... Everything."

I open my mouth again, and this time she presses her hand to my mouth. The radio starts cranking out a song by Color Green. This is so wrong. I mean, you won't find a bigger Color Green fan than me, but Todd Sparrow and the boys cranking out an angst ridden number is not what I need right now. Lia says:

"I'm sorry."

I can't quite figure out what for so I say:

"What for?"

"For leading you on. For making you think this afternoon that something could happen between us. I knew better, and I meant to tell you on the roof last night. But like you said, you took out a rack of Twinkies for me. No one has ever been such an idiot."

"It's okay. Still, I at least thought your mom would have told me. She seems like that kind of lady."

"She thought it was my place."

"Oh."

She takes my hand and puts her head on my shoulder. I lean my head on hers. We sit like this for a while. I don't know what I'm going to do. I guess there's not much I can do but keep on doing what I've always done. The doorbell rings.

She doesn't move. I say:

"So are you going down South to finish school?"

"I'm done with school."

"Oh. Where did you go?"

"Central."

"I went to Central. Why didn't I ever see you there? Did you transfer? I thought you meant that you were done with college."

"Are you delusional? I'm only seventeen. I got my GED last month. I wanted to get out of that asylum as soon as I could."

Before I can say anything Carol calls from downstairs:

"Jordan, it's someone for you."

This can't be good. I start for the door, then stop. I look at Lia:

"If you're leaving tomorrow why did you buy me the poster? How did you know you'd see me again?"

"I don't know."

CHAPTER THIRTEEN

After School Special

PAUL IS PACING FRANTICALLY AT the bottom of the steps.

"What are you doing here?"

"Looking for you. We've got problems." Paul looks like he's about to pass a small mammal through his urethra.

"What is it?" He doesn't say anything. I get the idea. I turn to Lia:

"Look, I'll come by later. Is that okay?"

"Yeah. Don't forget your board."

"I'll leave it here. That way I have an excuse," and I wink at her. She smirks.

On the porch Paul looks at me, then back at Lia's front door, and then hurries down the steps. I notice Lourdene's car is waiting on the curb.

"What's going on?"

"I'll explain it on the way."

"Where are we going? Don't you know the girl of my dreams is leaving tomorrow, possibly for good?" I pause to consider what I've just said. If I heard someone say that on television I would change the channel.

Paul gets in the car. I open the passenger door and say:

"What's going on?"

"Stop being such a bitch and get in the car. Megan tried to kill herself."

I get in the car. Paul slams the gas before I have my door shut. He runs the stop sign at the end of the street and turns onto Euclid and heads in the direction of University Hospital. I feel my bowels gurgle.

"What happened?"

Paul swerves around a car that's stopped at a red light and runs right through the intersection.

"Are you okay to drive?"

"Yeah. Anyway, after you left the shit really hit the fan. I went inside after you limped off, all the women were gathered around Megan, she was hysterical, and it's a good thing you were gone. I thought they were going to cut my dick off just because you were my friend. A fucking riot was about to ensue, and the frat boys, of course, were all about kicking your ass. I threw them out and Lara gave me shit for it, but I told her there was more to this because you were outside crying." He turns to me. "Sorry about that."

"It's okay."

"And then Megan spills it. I should have guessed, right? I didn't notice during any of this drama that Craig was in the corner white as a sheet. Anyway, Megan starts going on and on about how she loves you and didn't mean to hurt you, and how she tried to find a way to make you happy, and how she slept with a friend of yours. Well, I knew it wasn't me. And nothing personal here but you don't have any other friends. So I looked at Craig and he just nodded his head and I'm like, *Well this is a fine mess.* So Megan went to the bathroom. Who are we to stop her, right? I'm not a Goddamned suicide hotline. I can't see this shit coming. Next thing we know she's been in there for twenty minutes while we've all be grilling Craig, and Brenda goes and finds her doubled up on the floor holding her stomach."

"Christ."

"Yeah."

"What did she take? Fuck knows what you've got in the medicine cabinet."

"Well, that's the beauty of Paul. I don't keep drugs in easily accessible places for obvious reasons. I like to keep people away from my stash."

"So what did she take?"

"Are you ready for this? Aspirin and Ex-Lax."

I shake my head. This is serious. The girl tried to kill herself, over me, and I should be worried sick. Which I am. But I start to laugh. Paul smiles at me and then he starts laughing, too.

"She's going to be all right," he says. "They gave her something to slow her digestive system down so she wouldn't shit herself senseless. I think they gave her some serious Valium, too."

"Well, if she's going to be okay, why are you driving like this is life or death?"

"How often does something like this happen? It's fun."

* * *

I'm trying to get my straight face together. They've got Megan behind some curtains in the emergency room, and Brenda and Lara are in there talking to her. Paul has taken Lourdene outside so he can smoke and make my case to her so I don't go down as the bad guy. Despite Megan's earlier confession the women still see me as the destroyer of the world.

But I can't stop laughing. And not because of poor Megan. I'm touched that she felt losing me meant her life was over and that she might as well end it. There's a beauty to that act that is terribly classical. I have to resist the urge to throw back the curtains and gather her in my arms, kiss her and tell her that I still love her. How could I have done this to her, my sweet, forever love?

But she screwed Craig. Tough cookies.

Also, I'm laughing because when Paul and I arrived at the emergency room the woman at the reception desk was so precious about us, I guess, due to the fact that this was some After School Special teen suicide number. She was concerned that we were going to be tremendously upset. She asked us if we wanted anything, like a soda, and did we need to call our parents? Paul looked at her like she was nuts, but I thought it was nice that she wanted to help. I asked her if there was free counseling someplace and she gave me a card and walked off beaming. Sometimes people just need to be needed. Paul rolled his eyes at me.

Of course, perhaps I should chalk this giddiness up to nerves. I haven't been in a hospital since my mother's surgery, and the feeling that consumed me then was one of impending doom. I can't shake the image now of hospitals as places where people come to wait for bad news, or just to wait. At the time that was the worst, the waiting and wondering what was going to happen. And no one ever has answers. There was a point during mom's surgery when I wanted someone to tell me anything, even if it was horrible, just so I would know.

Lara and Brenda emerge from behind the curtains, and for once Brenda doesn't say a snide word to me. Instead, she brushes past me and Lara steps up to the plate:

"I hope you're fucking happy."

I purse my lips at her and do my best to look unamused.

"Lara, this isn't my fault. She slept with Craig."

"You think you can use that as an excuse? That girl loves you. I don't know why. What kind of sick motherfucker are you? People who love one another forgive one another. She tried to kill herself because of you. You disgust me."

Lara walks away. I don't think she should ever be allowed to make decisions that affect the lives of others; her reasoning is entirely suspect to me right now.

I pull back the curtains and Megan's eyes open halfway. She looks stoned out of her gourd.

"Baby," she says, and she lifts her arm like she's floating in a better place. I say:

"Hey," and I walk over and take her hand and stand beside her bed.

"I feel sleepy."

"I bet you do."

"You hate me."

I want to explain to her that *hate* isn't at all the right word. I'm hurt.

"No. I don't hate you."

"Yes you do."

I give her hand a squeeze and put my face close to hers:

"Meg, I'm not going to argue with you right now. I don't hate you. I'm worried about you."

She puckers her lips and closes her eyes. Kissing doesn't seem like the appropriate thing to do at the moment. But I don't think that rule still applies if someone has attempted, however feebly, to commit suicide.

I kiss her quickly. She says:

"You still love me?"

"Of course."

The words come so quickly from my mouth, so easily, it weirds me out. This chick fucked a friend of mine behind my back. (Yes, yes I know I was scoping out some other chick, but scoping and screwing are very different acts.)

But I do still love her, oddly enough. Forget the bad sex, which really isn't what it's all about (though I put a lot of stock in it). I mean this girl genuinely cares for me. She gave me her virginity, which I personally don't find to be that big of a deal, but she was raised Catholic and so she's condemned herself to the fires of hell for me. And she was willing to do it again by taking her own life. Granted, she didn't seem really invested in it, otherwise she might have gone a few steps further than analgesics and laxatives, but she still tried. She deserves better.

But she's just nineteen, so who can say how much of this has really been love and not just some stray hormones knocking around?

"Meg," I say, "get some rest. I'll be right here."

"Don't go," she says. "I'll die, please don't go."

"Meg, I'll be right here. Promise. You need to rest." I lean down and brush her hair our of her face and kiss her forehead. It breaks my heart.

She smiles, closes her eyes, and mumbles for me not to go. I watch her. Her breathing quickly falls into a heavy rhythm. I slip my hand out of hers and go back out into the waiting area. Paul is sitting by himself.

"Where did the girls go?"

"Outside. Trying to figure out how to best kill you and have it seem like an accident."

I shake my head.

"How's Megan?"

"Sleeping."

Paul nods. I sit down next to him and feel completely wiped out. I sigh, close my eyes. I feel like crashing hard. Paul puts his hand on my knee and gives it a squeeze. I say:

"What time is it?"

"Almost midnight."

I need to go to Lia's. I need to see her one last time. I don't know what I'll say to her. Maybe I'll tell her that I could have loved her forever. That I will, regardless.

What am I saying? I've known this girl for a few days and I'm making declarations of eternal love? I'm an idiot. And it's late. That's all I can figure. I didn't make any declarations of love to Megan for months, and only then when it looked like confessing it would bump me from hand job status to the first class section of vagina. Not that it really mattered, of course.

I look at Paul:

"Paul, I'm beat. I need to get home, and there's no way I'm getting in a car with those girls. Besides, I know they're staying, and I know I look like a bastard leaving, but man, it's been a rough night for me too. I just want to get cleaned up before I go see Lia and tell her good-bye. Can you spot me a few bucks for a cab?"

Before I've even finished my sentence, though, Paul is taking out his wallet. He says:

"I've only got a couple of bucks. Take my ATM card here and get some cash across the street and just drop it off tomorrow. My pin number is 'beer.' It's a savings account.

"Oh." This is a new concept to me. "Are you sure?" I don't like being trusted with Paul's ATM card since I've never used one.

"Take it. It'll be okay, fat cat. If anything happens I'll call you."

"You're a prince, man."

Paul waves it off. I take the card from his hand and head for the exit.

I'm paranoid about using the card at the teller machine on the street. I keep looking around me like any second some gang members are going to melt out of the shadows and have me empty out Paul's account. Not, of course, that there is a gang in Syracuse. I hate being an inexperienced ATM user.

I start to press the button to get twenty dollars from savings but I stop. I've always been slightly curious about how much money Paul has, exactly. I mean, I've asked him, but he always skirts around the question with an answer along the lines of 'enough.' I feel guilty about it; it's like fingering through someone's stuff when they're not home. Which everyone does. Besides, I can rationalize this by saying I need to know so I can assess how quickly Paul needs me to pay him back. I select 'balance inquiry' and wait. Best as I can figure he has a couple of grand left.

Which isn't the case at all. He only has twelve hundred dollars left. I wonder if he knows this? Paul never seems to be concerned about how much money he has. He's always been fairly generous with it. I go ahead and withdraw twenty bucks, then shove the money and the card in my pocket and toss the receipt on the ground.

CHAPTER FOURTEEN

Some Hallmark Hall of Fame Bullshit

ALL OF THE LIGHTS IN my house are on. This doesn't seem right. My parents' car is in the driveway which means dad is home. He should be at work right now.

I enter through the kitchen as always. Dad is sitting at the table with a series of papers spread out in front of him. Kelly is sitting silently beside him. She looks up at me and shakes her head. She stands and motions for me to follow her. I stop and look at what dad is doing as I pass by: he's painting water colors. My dad doesn't paint.

Kelly is waiting for me in my room.

"What's going on here?"

She doesn't speak but instead shuts the door to my room. I don't have the patience for this.

"Look, if something is up you've got to drop the silent treatment, okay? I don't feel like playing a game of charades to figure out what this is all about. I'm sorry you saw my penis, and I'm not any happier about that than you, but just get over it."

She takes a step towards me. I take a step back.

"I wasn't being quiet because I saw your dick. You are such an asshole. You don't have a clue what's going on do you?"

Something is wrong with mom. It makes sense now. The talk this afternoon doesn't seem so random after all. I can feel the tears starting to build, so I try to say what I can before they come flooding out. I collapse on the bed.

"What's wrong with her?"

Kelly seems to lose all of her anger at once and she sits down on the bed next to me.

"She's gone."

I start to sob uncontrollably. I feel myself start shaking. I didn't have a chance to tell her good-bye or thank her for the hamburger helper. I manage to choke out:

"When did it happen?"

"Tonight. A couple of hours ago."

While I was out screwing off with my own meaningless problems my mom was dying. I hate myself. I hate myself for not knowing, for not being here, for brushing her off this afternoon. I say:

"But she seemed fine this afternoon. Why didn't anyone call?"

"What was I supposed to do? I was having a tough enough time with dad. He went catatonic. Besides, she was gone by the time he got home from work."

"You were the only one with her?"

"And that fucker Rob."

I'm a little confused. I suck some snot up into my nose and

look at Kelly:

"Why was Rob here?"

"Because she left with him."

"What?"

"Are you high? Mom and dad's friend Rob have been having an affair. That's what's been bothering me for the last few days. I walked in on them the other night when mom thought I was staying at my boyfriend's."

I wipe my face, sit up.

"Mom and Rob are having an affair?"

"Yes!"

Rob is our godfather. He gives me ten dollars on Christmas and my birthday. He still goes to church. When mom was in the hospital and dad was staying with her all the time, Rob came over to the house and cooked Kelly and me dinner and made us do our homework. Rob is a saint. Rob couldn't be boning my mother. It doesn't make any sense.

And then I remember the pills in mom's purse. Kelly says:

"Apparently when dad was filling in for Rob refereeing boxing, Rob used that time to boink mom."

"Didn't you try to stop her? I mean, from leaving?"

"I haven't been speaking to her since the other night either. If she wants to go, she can go. And she did."

"Why didn't you tell me the other day?"

"Why? Look at you. I tell you mom's gone and you fall to pieces."

"I thought you meant she was dead."

"Oh. Well that makes a lot more sense then. I just thought you were a total douche bag or something."

"Yeah."

I get up and go down the hall to the bathroom, get some tissue and blow my nose, and then I poke my head into the kitchen. Dad is still at the water colors. He's lost it. I go back to my room. Kelly is flipping through a copy of *Hustler*. I take it from her and slide it back under my bed. She looks up at me:

"That stuff really turn you on?"

"Sometimes."

"But women aren't like that at all. Sex either. At least not any sex I've ever had. And I doubt Lia is like that."

"Yeah. I'd rather not talk about this."

"Why not? Does it bother you?"

"You're my little sister."

"I saw you masturbating."

I nod. I sit down on the bed beside her and I think about why I like *Hustler*. Certainly it's not for the articles. Maybe it's because I wish sex could be like those pictures, just wild and nasty, but I had that tonight with Megan and look how that turned out. The most genuine part of my evening was sitting and kissing and talking with Lia. I never thought anything like that could be so intimate. Even when Megan and I had what I would describe as a relatively good encounter it was always like, *Okay, here's your orgasm, now here's mine, thank you, please drive through*. There was a wall between us. It was never like we were there for each other, but for ourselves, and we just needed someone else to help finish the job. It's sad actually. I think about all the copies of *Hustler* and other mags under my bed, all the pictures of people copulating, and it's suddenly very unappealing. I look at Kelly.

"I don't know why I'm turned on by them. They're really depressing."

She doesn't say anything. I let out a sigh:

"So how long has dad been painting?"

"Not long after he got home. When I called him at work I didn't say what had happened, only that there was an emergency. When he came in I told him that mom was gone. He went to his room and shut the door. I thought he was going to kill himself."

"What did you do?"

"Nothing. That's his right. Anyway, he came out a few minutes later with a   little water color kit and he's been painting since then."

"Should we call a doctor or something? He's off his rocker."

"I don't think so. The paintings are actually pretty good."

I stand and begin pacing back and forth.

"So you just walked in on mom and Rob the other day? What happened?"

"Nothing really. Rob ran down the hall and mom pulled on her robe and asked me if I was hungry. I just turned and walked out."

"Where were they?"

"In the kitchen."

"Christ."

"Please don't pace. It's distracting."

"Distracting? From what? From the fact that our mother ran off with our godfather? From the fact that dad just suddenly started painting? How can anything distract you from that?"

"It just does."

I shake my head. I can't believe this. I sit back down on the bed. I say to Kelly:

"Well, what do we do now?"

"I don't know."

This doesn't help me much. I'm going to go and talk to dad. I tell her:

"I'm going to go and talk to dad."

"Good luck."

"Yeah."

I stand up. Kelly stands up, too. I don't know why—maybe it's because we share the same DNA—but we both move to hug one another at the same time. I squeeze her tight. It's been so long since I've hugged her. I'd forgotten what it was like to have a sister.

But I have to let her go. Dad needs me right now. I turn and walk down the hall and into the kitchen where dad is. I sit next to him. He doesn't look at me. I'm not sure where to begin, so I just look at the paintings he has in front of him.

There are two that are complete; he's working on a third. And they are pretty good. I mean what do I know about art? But these are certainly better than the crap you might find hanging on the walls in the dentist's office. One is a nature scene: ducks flying over two islands in a marsh. The second is a guy leaning on his pickup truck that's parked in front of an old general store. I'm amazed by the detail, the store front with the sign and cracks in the wood.

But the one he's currently working on is of a woman reclining topless on a couch—and it's absolutely beautiful. She's looking away from you, so you can just see the curve of her cheek, and her breasts are perfect, and the curve of her hips and thighs... But there's something about her breasts. I stare at them. It's a few minutes before I get it. I look at the other two paintings and how the islands and the tires on the truck each look like the woman's breasts from a different angle. Oh, dad. I say:

"Dad, I'm sorry."

He doesn't respond. I feel that I should tell him that I know that he loved mom, and I know he's hurting more than he could ever begin to explain. I want to let him know that he shouldn't be ashamed to cry in front of us, and that if he feels suicidal he should talk to someone. But dad and I have never talked that way. We're never open. If we were it would be just one more sign that the world is spiraling toward oblivion. So instead of all that emotional, feel-good crap I say:

"I didn't know you painted."

"You probably wouldn't remember. I did it a lot when you and your sister were young. The first few years *you* were around anyway. That's all I did before you were born. I was going to go to art school. But things went a different way. You know."

This is all news to me. I didn't know dad ever wanted to do anything else. I've always speculated that his life as I've known it wasn't his dream, but art school? I never would have guessed. I say:

"These are good."

He ignores me.

"Why did you start painting?"

"It's very therapeutic."

I'm not sure if he's talking about why he started painting tonight or just in general but I don't care. The way he says it—there's a certain sadness in his voice. But there is also a resolve as if he's trying to tell me he'll be okay. I wish I had something more to say to him.

"Dad, if you need anything, I'm here."

"Why don't you get a job and move out of my house. You're twenty years old."

I get up and go back to my room.

Along both walls of the hallway mom has hung family pictures. I've gotten used to them over the years, like the knick-knacks sprinkled throughout the house, so I hardly even notice them anymore.

But I can't ignore them now. They are these awful things. There's this one picture where dad has mom thrown over his shoulder and they're laughing—it was clearly taken before I was born. I always liked this picture because it was mom and dad in a way I never saw them: completely in love. But I almost can't bear to look at it now. I don't think either of them imagined their lives turning out to be like this, hovering just above the poverty line continually, mom having cancer, she and dad drifting apart, and then her night flight with Rob.

I guess this sudden turn of events answers the question of what I most want to know.

I don't suppose I can really blame mom for leaving since she and dad stopped touching or talking, and because Kelly and I aren't really around that much, what was here for her? She didn't have a life. I usually think about the cancer as nearly taking her life, but I guess it did anyway in a certain sense.

Right beside mom and dad's bedroom door there's a picture of dad holding me as a newborn just after they brought me home from the hospital. Dad is smiling at the camera, and I'm looking up at him, and the look on my face is the weirdest thing. I don't look happy, or upset, or like I've got gas, but just like I'm thinking. I wonder what I was thinking and what was happening in my baby head? Was I trying to make sense of everything after having been yanked from mom's belly? That picture doesn't seem to give any indication that my life would become what it is, that I'd be stuck. (Inert, I guess, would be the word.) Lia was right: to glimpse into my infant brain would be another world, the beginning of a world with different possibilities. I consider all the lives I could have lived starting from that point and branching out and how truly unknowable they all are...

I shift my weight from one foot to the next while looking at the pictures on the wall and the floor makes an awful creaking I've never noticed. I'm reminded of Lia's ski lifts, about the things meant for something and then left without a purpose.

I look again at the picture of dad holding me. What was I meant for?

Kelly is sitting on my bed looking at *Hustler* again. She looks up as I enter the room:

"Most of the breasts in this magazine aren't real."

"Of course not. Don't be silly."

"What did he say?"

"Not much. He wanted to go to art school before we were born."

"I didn't know that."

"Look, I need to clear my head. This night has been a mess. Megan tried to kill herself, and now this thing with mom..."

"Megan did what?"

"Yeah, long story. I don't feel much like going into it. She banged Craig, I told her it was over, she flipped."

"She tried to kill herself over you? I always thought that girl was an idiot."

I frown.

"I'm going for a walk. Hold down the fort."

Kelly frowns back at me.

"Yeah. I'll make sure that things remain calm and normal around here. That shouldn't be hard at all."

CHAPTER FIFTEEN

In Motion

THE DEEP THUMP OF BASS emanating from No Borders is audible at the corner of Marshall Street and University Place. I considered walking back over to Lia's and confessing everything to her, but what chick wants that when she's just met a guy? The last thing anybody wants is extra baggage. Although this emotional turmoil could be made into a case for a sympathy lay...

But I don't want to bag Lia on sympathy just hours before she leaves. In fact, I'm not looking to bag her at all. I'm genuinely sad that she's leaving when I've finally started making head way. Seriously: finding the perfect girl who is leaving town in a few hours, current girlfriend trying to kill herself, mom running off into the night with your godfather...? If my life was a book I wouldn't believe it. But I don't really read anyway so it doesn't matter.

It also occurred to me to go by the hospital and see how Meg is doing, and to fill Paul in on the utter bullshit that I walked into back at the house. But I don't want to deal with any of that right now either.

In fact, I don't want to deal with anything. I feel like I've had a year's worth of emotional trauma dumped on me in the last 24 hours and I deserve a break.

Have you had your break today? I wonder if Dean Peterson was humming that to himself as his Pinto was loaded with overly processed fish and chicken? It kind of takes on a whole new meaning when you think about it.

A guy I went to high school with, Gus, is standing outside No Borders looking ultra-cool and distracted. He's about 6'5" with a lean build and a thick blond mane down to his ass. He's known for his massages and bass playing. I've often wondered if the two are connected. As I approach him he turns to me and says:

"Jordan. You seen any hairy girls? I mean *really* hairy. Like, furry."

"No, Gus, I sure haven't. But I'll send them your way."

"Please do. I love me some hairy women."

Gus grunts and does a little break dance move and then resumes his pose. I start up the stairs. It smells like weed and cigarettes and sweat. It seems like the best place possible to forget everything. The pulse of the music feels like it is already shaking the worry and dread from me. It feels good. I feel like dancing. I don't feel this way often because to be honest I hate people who dance. I hate the little pretentious pricks on the dance floor trying to be the center of attention. However, right now I'm willing to make some concessions on my personal convictions in exchange for some sort of release.

An arm blocks me as I crest the stairs:

"Ten bucks man."

"Sure." I reach into my pocket: nothing. Then I remember that I took a cab form the hospital to my house earlier. "Hey man, I'm a little short right now. Think you could let me slide? I'm up here all the time and I've had a bitch of a day."

"Sorry man. I've already let too many people slide. Maybe you can find some people down on the street who will spot you, but my hands are tied. I don't mean to be a dick. You know how it is."

"Yeah, I know how it is. The whole fucking world is against me—that's how it is. This is how Pintos end up in McDonald's."

"I hear you, man. Right on."

I turn and head back down the steps. All I want to do is dance. The one time in forever I've felt like dancing and the cosmos can't cut me a break. I'm beginning to wonder what I've done to deserve all this. I can't think of anything. In the past few years I've done absolutely nothing, and you can't be punished for that can you? I always thought karma was something you racked up by evil deeds, and I've been extremely careful in my life to walk a very fine and neutral line. It just doesn't make any sense. Gus says:

"Wassup, my man?"

"The cover."

"That sucks, my brother." Gus reaches out and grabs my shoulders and starts rubbing. I'm not hip on being massaged by another dude, but I must confess Gus has the magic touch.

"Gus, I've had about the worst day ever."

"How so?"

"I found out my girlfriend slept with another guy, then tried to kill herself because I was pissed about it; my mom ran off with my godfather; and I've met this other girl who just—Gus, there's never been another girl like her, ever—and she's leaving on a bus tomorrow."

Gus is quiet. He kneads my shoulders a little harder. I go:

"And I don't know why all this is coming down on me. I haven't done anything. None of this has anything to do with me, except that I bear the brunt of the consequences."

I lean my head down as Gus rubs my neck and I shove my hands in my back pockets out of confusion with what to do with them. I feel Paul's ATM card against my fingers. I'm sure if Paul were here he wouldn't mind forking out a little cash for a good time to be had.

"Gus, I'll be right back. I just found my ticket in."

First thing I do is grab a bottle of water from Sara who's working behind the counter and ask her who The Man is.

"See that guy over there with the chain?"

"Yeah."

"See him."

I go over to the kid with the chain that connects his wallet to his belt loop.   I say:

"Sara says you're The Man."

"Let's step into the back."

I follow him past the DJ spinning records and into a small room that Sara uses as an office. Some people are crashed out on a couch passing a blunt back and forth.

"What you need?"

"What you got?"

The Man removes his backpack and unzips it and peers inside:

"Rolls, shrooms, weed, valium, liquid, and I know someone who has coke."

"I'll take three rolls, a couple caps, an eighth of weed, and some valium for later."

"You sound serious."

"I've had a bad day."

The Man cocks his head to the side and raises an eyebrow at me.

"You know, I have a personal policy of not dealing to people who are in a self-destructive state. It's a bad business practice."

"I'm not self-destructive. I just want to forget myself for a while."

"You know your problems will still be there in the morning, right?"

"Are you a fucking *Just Say No* ad or what?"

"What I'm saying is that I don't just dole out chemicals to the general populace. That's how drugs get a bad rap."

I look past The Man to the kids zonked out of their heads on the couch.

"I'm sure you have the best intentions, and I'm sure you're used to dealing with the highest quality clientele, but you see, I'm in a bad way here. My folks just split up, this girl I've been seeing—"

The Man zips his backpack and throws it over his shoulder in a fluid motion that has the dramatic touch of finality to it.

"Look, nothing personal here, but I don't have a good feeling about you. You've got some heavy vibrations and I don't think you should be using drugs as an escape from that right now."

"You're kidding me."

"No." He pushes past me and stops at the door. "This stuff with the family and the girl—you bring any of this on yourself?"

"What? No. What kind of a question is that?"

"Well, I've never seen anyone look as guilty as you in my life. You need to work on that."

I watch him go out into the blue hue of light in the coffee shop, disappearing amongst the pulsing, sweaty bodies.

"Hey man."

I turn around and one of the waste-oids on the couch is holding out the blunt to me.

"What?"

"I got a couple pills if you want them."

"What are they?"

"Something... what was it? I don't know... it shoots you into the nether regions."

He pulls out a little pill bottle. I give him $40 for two. He offers me a hit off the blunt. I join him and his companions on the couch and wait to see what happens.

I am a Mechanical Man, I am a Mechanical Man, I am a Mechanical Man. It's that Charles Manson Song. It's in my head and I can't get it out. A lot of people don't know that Charles Manson wrote music. I never bought any because I never thought it was that good, but Chris Ward owned it on cassette and he used to play it all the time before he got hit by that car. I remember the first time I heard that song about being a mechanical man and afterwards it wouldn't leave my head. It's like that now: stuck. Also most people don't know that Charles Manson auditioned to be one of the Monkees. Probably would have been a lot cooler if he had made the cut.

I am a Mechanical Man. That line has a beat. It's like four deliberate thumps, like the music the DJ is spinning. *Domp domp domp domp* over and over and over and over. It's in my head. I can feel it in my throat and chest, like the words and the music are inside me circulating and boiling and trying to get out. I'm on the couch. I need to be off the couch. Everything is blue light and red light and blurred bodies and motion and it's all bleeding together. I give up. There's no focus—just a big porridge of people. *Domp domp domp domp.* My legs are Jell-O. Watch them wiggle. I must move.

The Learning Channel teaches us that music is sacred because it is rhythm and sound at its purest—it existed before words. It is breath in the lungs, it is the beating of the heart, it is the essence of that which make us alive. The pumping of blood is bass and drums; the breath is horn and strings. Sound communicates without signs. It's *Close Encounters of the Third Kind.* I never realized how good that movie was until now. I love myself for liking that movie. I am all things Richard Dreyfuss and Disney right now. I am in love with the mystery of sound. It is holy.

When my dad finally broke down and bought a VCR that was the first movie he rented. It put me to sleep. I wanted to rent *Enter the Ninja*, but nobody cared what I wanted. I remember that mountain, that tune, the flying saucer. It was everything The Learning Channel says the world could be: it was joy beyond words. My own world is pretty far from that right now. Personally, I think I need a bigger boat. My legs are Jell-O. Watch them jiggle. I need to sit down.

I'm on a different couch with different people. I have my water. Sweat is dripping off me. Nothing seems real. Everything seems too real. *Domp domp domp domp*. It's still happening outside of me and in me. I feel like I am splitting atoms when I move. Was the word God? I remember that from the Bible. Or was God the word? I don't recall. I think God was sound. The Learning Channel says King James fucked up a lot of stuff. I think the *sound* was God. I think sound is vibration and everything vibrates. Things are solid because the atoms that make them are vibrating slower than other atoms. Did you know that if you could speed up the vibration of your atoms you could pass through solid objects? I read that in *The Flash*, although it wasn't the Flash that everyone thinks of because he was a bit before my time. When Kid Flash became the Flash after the Flash died in *Crisis on Infinite Earths*—that's when I picked up the story.

I wonder if I could make myself vibrate fast enough to pass from this Earth to the next one, if there is such a place of possibility, where things are happening altogether differently, where maybe I have a job and better options.

I have to move.

Atoms around me are smashing into me. My head is vibrating faster than my body can take it. There are monks, Zen monks I think, who learn how to sing an entire chord all by themselves. They believe that there is a sound which holds the universe together, and to sing the right sound is to... I can't remember. Something happens. Of course something happens. You're singing the sound that holds the universe in place, you are vibrating with the oneness of everything. Maybe you vanish in a cloud of smoke and spectacular fireworks, like you're the One Millionth Customer.

I am trying to vibrate as fast as my head. I'm not getting anywhere. Maybe I can't go that fast. I want to go fast enough to get the words out of my head and forget them. I want to purge. When did all this happen, all these words and burdens that slowed me down? Now I know why my dad moves so slow. I thought it was mom's sickness. Afterwards, dad moved slower, mom moved faster. They were suddenly in different orbits, like that tumor took a great weight from her and she was free.

I'm really fucked up.

I've got to tell someone.

"Hey man, I'm really fucked up."

"Right on, man." I can't even put a face with the voice.

The Learning Channel says that babies, when they're born, can't make out shapes. Everything is a big blur. Parents who think that babies know their face are idiots. Babies respond to sound. It's the sound of the voice, or the heart they know from the womb that soothes them. Why do you think that babies like to be held close to your breast? It's the heart they want to hear, not the emulation of feeding. They want to feed off of the sound, off the movement of breath and blood. Like all these people here, this big blur of blue light bodies, of atoms smashing, the stupid bliss of human noise all packed into to this sweaty room. We are undeniable. We are the glue holding it together, my blue collar father and his giant vibrating factory machines that make tiny machines that stir the atoms in the air to cool the atoms of your body, my mom and her monotonous office machines always making copies. I am their little mechanical man. We're moving but not going anywhere. Something in us isn't stirring. Not like now. Not like this. All these people, like me, we're moving now, the beat of the music, like a beat of a heart, reminds us of something. It is joy. It is movement in the mind. We have been acted upon. I get it now. I get it now. I get it now. I get it now.

CHAPTER SIXTEEN

Still Moving

PLEASE KILL ME.

I'm on my hands and knees in the bushes outside my house, trying to decide if I need to puke again. I woke up about an hour ago lying in my own vomit behind a couch in a corner of No Borders. Another breakfast of champions.

The walk home (without a shirt, mind you) was a series of humiliating moments retching into trash cans, bushes, and recycling bins. I think I'm done.

The house is straight up: *It's quiet. Too quiet.* It feels dead.

I'm unable to put anything together from last night, but a few things are certain: this is not the place I want to be right now. And it's not just my mom leaving, or Lia leaving, or Meg doped up in some hospital room. It's everything. It's this town. It's my friends. I love them all, but I just want to scream. If I stay here I feel like no one is going to hear me.

I open the cabinet above the refrigerator and find a bottle of Pepto. I drink some down and then put it on the counter. This little puppy is coming with me for sure. I pick up the phone.

I don't know Lia's last name. That's a tremendous oversight on my part. The clock on the microwave says seven-thirty. I run the math in my head. It does not compute. I am a wasted piece of crap. Totally cracked-out.

"You smell like shit."

Kelly is in the doorway behind me rubbing her eyes.

"I feel like it, too."

"Paul called here for you last night."

"Did you tell him anything?"

"Yeah, I told him not to wake my ass up ever again by calling here so late."

I sigh. She softens.

"No. I thought you should tell him."

"Thanks."

I walk past her and back into my room. She follows me.

"So where did you go last night?"

"Out for a walk." I grab a shirt off the floor and throw it on. No time for a shower.

"Through the dumpsters? You look it."

I stare at my posters on the wall, my unfinished testament to nothing in particular. I turn to Kelly:

"Look, I'm getting out. I'm going to ask dad if I can borrow some of that money he was saving for mom's breasts."

"She took it all."

"What?"

My life blows. Kelly says:

"What do you mean you're getting out? You're leaving?"

"Yeah."

"Do you know how selfish that is?"

I grab my backpack from the closet and start putting clothes in it. Some t-shirts, shorts, underwear, the usual. I also take my dugout that holds about an eighth of weed. I walk down the hall to the bathroom to get my toothbrush. Kelly follows me. She says:

"What am I supposed to do? I can't take care of dad."

I take my toothbrush, and then decide I might as well take the toothpaste, too. Kelly snatches it from my hand. I look at her:

"You don't need to take care of him."

"Well, then what?"

I feel that this is bordering on a touching moment in which I tell Kelly that I love her but that she must now take care of herself. And yet:

"Look, you slut—give me that toothpaste and get out of my face."

"Prick."

I go for the toothpaste. In the process I drop my toothbrush in the toilet. I stop and look at it. Kelly erupts in laughter.

I grab her toothbrush and sling it in the toilet with mine. She doesn't do anything.

"That was dad's."

As if the man hasn't had enough, I throw his toothbrush in the toilet. I grab the last toothbrush in the rack and chuck it in the bowl. She says:

"That does it."

She makes a grab for a can of mousse, with the intention, I imagine, of dousing me with it. I intercept her and push her out into the hallway and start trying to wrestle the toothpaste from her hand. I don't know why. I mean, I don't have anything to use it with now except my finger, but it's a point of honor. I'm not leaving this house without it. I grab her nipple and twist, and she lets go, and I get a hold of the paste and start to head back to my room to grab my bag. But she knees me in the crotch and I drop.

"Jordan, you can leave if you want, but you're not getting this toothpaste. You hear me, puss-boy?"

I leg sweep her. It's cruel—maybe not as cruel as twisting her nipple, but it could certainly hurt her a lot more. I roll her over and pin her arms. Unfortunately, this leaves me without the ability to take the toothpaste from her. She looks up at me:

"I'm going to rip your nuts off."

"Try it."

Dad comes walking out of his room. He looks down at us and Kelly and I look at him. I'm waiting for him to punt me off of her. I know he'd still take his belt to me without even blinking an eye, regardless of my age. Kelly says:

"Dad, Jordan's trying to take the toothpaste."

"Dad," I say, "I'm leaving. I'm going to get a job and move out and I need this toothpaste."

He doesn't say a word. He reaches down and takes the toothpaste from Kelly's hand and goes into the bathroom and shuts the door. I get off of Kelly. I help her up and I go to my room and get my bag.

I turn off the light as I leave.

"Goddammit!" Dad screams from the bathroom. I make a dash for the door.

At the end of the driveway I turn and look at the house. I suddenly remember a Bible story where some woman turned to salt when she turned around and looked back when she wasn't supposed to. I head quickly down the street.

I notice that for the first time in days it doesn't feel humid. I am, in fact, a little chilly. I push my hands into my pockets and feel Paul's ATM card. I forgot about that. I need to borrow some money from Paul. That's just one more thing I have to worry about, besides getting another toothbrush.

But I don't even know how much I need. And I don't know where I'm going or how much things will cost when I get there. This is a lot more complicated than I thought. In the movies people just go, but it isn't like that in real life. There are problems that have to be worked around.

Fucking fuck.

I take a deep breath and mount the steps to Lia's front door and ring the bell. I pace around. I can't stand still. This is something totally new to me. I ring the bell again. I'm impatient. I open the screen door to knock on the main door and my board and the Descendents poster falls out at my feet. I'm too late.

I grab the board and the poster and jump down the steps. I slap the board down and hop on. It doesn't go anywhere. I try to run it back and forth with my foot to see if it's caught on a piece of gravel or something, but I get the same stiff results. I pick it up—the shoelace is still tangled around one of the wheels. And it's in there tight. I start walking over to Paul's.

I think about just shoving the ATM card under the door but it doesn't seem right. I want to tell Paul good-bye. He is, after all, my best friend.

I knock loudly. I hear Paul inside charging down the steps and he throws open the front door:

"What the fuck are you doing?"

"What?"

"Why didn't you just walk in?"

I didn't even think about that. I say:

"How's Megan?"

"She's fine. We took her home about an hour ago. I tried to call you."

"Kelly said as much. What did Meg's parents say?"

"I let the girls handle that. I didn't want any part of it."

"Understandable."

"Come on in. Let's have a morning bowl."

"I can't. I'm taking a trip with my family. We're about to leave. I totally flaked on it until this morning."

"Shit. You still have to do that stuff?"

"Well, yeah, you know. It's the first one since mom had surgery."

Paul nods his head:

"Oh. Well, that's cool then. I just thought that if it was some annual family outing then, well, you know..."

"Yeah."

Silence.

Then:

"Anyway, here's your card. Thanks."

"No problem. When will you be back?"

"You know, I'm not really sure."

"Why do you have that bag?"

"It's for the trip."

"Why isn't it in your folks' car?"

He knows. Paul's not stupid. Christ, I wanted to tell him thanks for all that he's done, and that I plan on paying him back the money I owe him, including the $400 that I withdrew before going to Lia's, but I can't do that now. I have to get out of here. I say:

"Paul, I have to go," and I stick out my hand.

He looks at it for the longest time, then he says:

"Have a good trip," and he shuts the door. I can't believe he wouldn't even shake my hand. Maybe he thought it was just utter cruelty for me to try and be cordial when I am obviously screwing him over, but it wasn't that at all: I wanted to shake his hand for everything before this, because he's been the best friend I could ever hope for. As I'm walking away I hear the door lock.

There's only one bus out of this town and Lia is on it and I'm going to be on it too. Though it does occur to me that Lia might not even want me to come with her. Well, it's too late for all of that now. The way I see it, if I stay here, my life will go on as always: I will walk by the same houses everyday, see the same friends, develop brand loyalty, grow impatient with new music, intolerant of new faces, become constipated when the mail is delivered later than usual or the paper doesn't come. And every cell in my body tells me that the move toward that kind of stability is the way to go. Twenty years of that kind of life being hammered into me day after day has done some damage.

However, if there's one thing I've picked up from The Learning Channel it's this: the universe is an unstable vacuum, but the basic nature of the cosmos is the desire to be stable. And if all that blackened void flickering with a touch of life here and there suddenly did that, we'd all be gone, without a sound. Which is something else to worry about: any second, quicker than you could draw a breath, we're finished, and none of it ever mattered. If that doesn't make you shudder listening to the garbage truck rattle down your street every Tuesday morning, well, I don't know what will. We are meant to thrive amidst instability and chance and possibility.

Or so the guy narrating that Learning Channel program says.

An old man is coming towards me, a small dog on a leash seeming to pull him forward. He gives me a look and I say:

"Hey, what time is it?"

"Nine-ten."

I might not make it. My life might just end up here, and this is where I'll die, because I know that if I don't get on that bus with her I don't have it in me to do it by myself. I tuck my board and poster under my arm. If I'm going to make it I'll have to run.

A Note on the Author

Kevin Keck is the author of *My Summer Vacation: Poems 1994-2004* and *B-Sides: Poems 1994-2014;* the memoirs *Oedipus Wrecked* and *Are You There God? It's Me. Kevin.*; and the anthology *Hard Evidence: the Collected Bawdy Writings.* He lives in North Carolina. Visit him at www.thekeck.org.